CASCA...

Timber Falls Cloaked in Mystery as Rainy Season Begins

by Charity Jenkins

Sheriff Mitch Tanner had his hands full when just hours before the rainy season began Bigfoot was spotted on the edge of town by our local bread delivery man. This is not the first Bigfoot sighting here—nor the last—but the real mystery is the disappearance of Dennison Ducks decoy painter Nina Monroe! The sheriff refused to confirm reports that foul play might have been involved, but one source said Nina's boss, Wade Dennison, was very upset when she didn't show for work this morning. Nina has been in town for only a month and little is known about her. But never fear, this reporter will get to the bottom of it....

Dear Harlequin Intrigue Reader,

The holidays are upon us! We have six dazzling stories of intrigue that will make terrific stocking stuffers—not to mention a well-deserved reward for getting all your shopping done early....

Take a breather from the party planning and unwrap Rita Herron's latest offering, *A Warrior's Mission*—the next exciting installment of COLORADO CONFIDENTIAL, featuring a hot-blooded Cheyenne secret agent! Also this month, watch for *The Third Twin*—the conclusion of Dani Sinclair's HEARTSKEEP trilogy that features an identical triplet heiress marked for murder who seeks refuge in the arms of a rugged lawman.

The joyride continues with *Under Surveillance* by highly acclaimed author Gayle Wilson. This second book in the PHOENIX BROTHERHOOD series has an undercover agent discovering that his simple surveillance job of a beautiful woman-in-jeopardy is filled with complications. Be there from the start when B.J. Daniels launches her brand-new miniseries, CASCADES CONCEALED, about a close-knit northwest community that's visited by evil. Don't miss the first unforgettable title, *Mountain Sheriff*.

As a special gift-wrapped treat, three terrific stories in one volume. Look for *Boys in Blue* by reader favorites Rebecca York, Ann Voss Peterson and Patricia Rosemoor about three long-lost New Orleans cop brothers who unite to reel in a killer. And rounding off a month of nonstop thrills and chills, a pregnant woman and her wrongly incarcerated husband must set aside their stormy past to bring the real culprit to justice in *For the Sake of Their Baby* by Alice Sharpe.

Best wishes to all of our loyal readers for a joyous holiday season!

Enjoy,

Denise O'Sullivan
Senior Editor
Harlequin Intrigue

MOUNTAIN SHERIFF
B.J. DANIELS

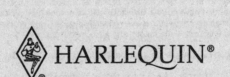

HARLEQUIN®

TORONTO • NEW YORK • LONDON
AMSTERDAM • PARIS • SYDNEY • HAMBURG
STOCKHOLM • ATHENS • TOKYO • MILAN • MADRID
PRAGUE • WARSAW • BUDAPEST • AUCKLAND

ISBN 0-373-22744-2

MOUNTAIN SHERIFF

This edition published by arrangement with Harlequin Books S.A.

® and TM are trademarks of the publisher. Trademarks indicated with ® are registered in the United States Patent and Trademark Office, the Canadian Trade Marks Office and in other countries.

Visit us at www.eHarlequin.com

Printed in U.S.A.

ABOUT THE AUTHOR

A former award-winning journalist, B.J. Daniels had thirty-six short stories published before her first romantic suspense, *Odd Man Out,* came out in 1995. B.J. lives in Montana with her husband, Parker, two springer spaniels, Zoey and Scout, and a temperamental tomcat named Jeff. She is a member of Kiss of Death, the Bozeman Writers Group and Romance Writers of America. When she isn't writing, she snowboards in the winters and camps and boats in the summers. All year she plays her favorite sport, tennis. To contact her, write: P.O. Box 183, Bozeman, MT 59771 or visit her Web site at www.bjdanielsweb.com.

Books by B.J. Daniels

HARLEQUIN INTRIGUE

*Cascades Concealed

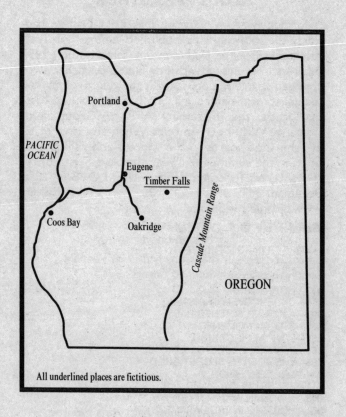

PACIFIC
OCEAN

Portland

Eugene
Timber Falls

Coos Bay

Oakridge

Cascade Mountain Range

OREGON

All underlined places are fictitious.

CAST OF CHARACTERS

Charity Jenkins—She's set her sights on confirmed bachelor Sheriff Mitch Tanner—and the newspaper story she's working on could get her killed.

Mitch Tanner—The rainy season in Timber Falls is always bad, but this year it starts with a murder.

Nina Monroe—The duck-decoy painter lied about who she was and why she was in town—and now she's gone missing.

Wade Dennison—The owner of Dennison Ducks is hiding something. But is it murder?

Daisy Dennison—She became a recluse when her baby daughter, Angela, was stolen from her crib twenty-seven years ago.

Angela Dennison—Twenty-seven years ago Angela was stolen from her crib and never seen again.

Alma Bromdale—The nanny had been sleeping soundly in the room next to Angela's…

Desiree Dennison—For years she's had to live in her missing younger sister's shadow. The last thing she wants is Angela to turn up now in the flesh.

Jesse Tanner—Is it just a coincidence that Mitch's outlaw older brother shows up in Timber Falls now?

Ethel Whiting—She knows the Dennison family better than anyone in town. Maybe too well.

Sheryl Bends—Did the painter hate Nina Monroe enough for stealing one of her duck designs that she could have killed her?

Bud Farnsworth—The production manger at Dennsion Ducks has a chip on his shoulder and a mean temper.

Kyle L. Rogers—The P.I. doesn't know it, but he was hired to make sure the kidnapper's identity stays a secret.

This book is dedicated with much appreciation to JoAnn Brehm. Thank you for sharing your stories about life in Oregon and the long rainy season.

Oregon is a beautiful, diverse state and one I found both fascinating and a little mystifying. Especially in the deepest, darkest woods on the rain shadow side of the Cascades, where it takes little imagination to believe that Bigfoot watches from the shadows.

Chapter One

Darkness pressed against the window. Beyond the glass, something moved at the edge of the tangle of growth.

Under the glow of the desk lamp, Nina Monroe feathered the paint along one side of the wooden duck decoy.

She'd forgotten she was alone in the isolated Dennison Ducks decoy plant. Nor had she noticed how late it was. Her mind had been on her future.

For the first time in her twenty-seven years of life, her future looked good. Not just good. Dazzling. Almost blinding. Sometimes she had to pinch herself it was so hard to believe. Soon she would have everything she'd ever wanted. Soon she wouldn't be painting duck decoys in the middle of nowhere, that was for sure.

A voice in her head warned her not to count her chickens before they'd hatched. The voice was that of her old-maid aunt Harriet and she shut it out, just as she had all of her life. Aunt Harriet the doomsayer.

After tonight, Nina would finally have what she deserved. It had been a long time coming. She smiled at the thought of blowing this dinky boring town knowing she'd never look back, never even give Timber Falls, Oregon, another thought. She felt dazed by the possibilities. And filled with righteous indignation that it had taken so long for justice to finally be done.

She'd picked Halloween. A perfect time to unmask the true villains. By Halloween, she'd be long gone— but not forgotten. She would have it all, the money— *and*—the revenge. Who said revenge wasn't sweet?

A noise at the window made her look up. From the darkness appeared a distorted face. It filled the window, the eyes like empty sockets.

She let out a strangled cry, dropping her paintbrush as she shoved back her chair and stumbled to her feet.

Just as suddenly as it had appeared, the face was gone. She snapped off the lamp, the only light in her corner of the decoy plant, and stood in the dark staring out at the night.

Beyond the glass was a jungle of ferns, vines, moss and trees that fought for space in the suffocating rain forest on the Pacific Ocean side of the Oregon Cascades. Sometimes she felt so closed in here she wanted to scream.

Like right now. The trees moved restlessly in the wind. Shadows flickered over the glass from what little moonlight pierced the forest.

She took a breath and tried to calm herself. There was no one out there. It had just been a trick of moonlight and shadows. Hadn't her life always been full of shadows? But not for much longer.

So close to finally getting everything she wanted, she felt nervous, jittery, excited and maybe a little spooked. Spooked because something could go wrong.

But she knew that was just her aunt Harriet talking. After all those years with the pessimistic old woman, Nina could hear Harriet in her head. The voice of negativity. The voice of defeat.

She pushed all thoughts of Harriet away as she looked out the window again and saw nothing but the movement of trees and ferns in the faint moonlight.

Glancing at her watch, with its glowing dial, Nina saw that she had at least another hour to wait. She wanted to try to finish this duck decoy, hating to admit that over the past month, she'd come to enjoy the painting.

It required an exactness that appealed to her. She'd found she had a talent for it that surprised—and pleased—her.

From behind her, she heard a soft click. The sound of the door, on the other side of the building, opening?

She turned slowly. A single small bulb illuminated the employee entrance, casting the dark images of hundreds of ducks over her. Mallard and canvasback, pintail and greenwing, buffalohead and widgeon decoys filled the shelves from the floor to ceiling.

From where she stood, she couldn't see past the shelves covered with ducks. Had she imagined the sound, just as she'd imagined the face at the window?

"Sure, that's all it was," she could hear Aunt Harriet sneer. "Fool."

Something moved across the light on the other side of the building. A flicker of dark shadow followed by the soft scuff of a shoe on concrete. The scent of damp night air cut through the sweeter scent of freshly carved pine. She heard another click. The door closing?

It was too early. Unless there'd been a change in plans. But then, wouldn't she have gotten a call? After all, tonight was supposed to be the last time they would meet. Once she had the money…

She glanced up at Wade Dennison's second-story glassed-in office, half expecting to see the owner of the plant watching her as he so often did. But the office was dark, just as she knew it would be, and there was no one behind the glass.

Another soft scuff of a shoe, closer this time. She told herself it had to be one of the employees. No one else had a key to get in. Unless in her excitement she'd forgotten to lock the door.

Her heart lodged in her throat as she frantically tried to remember locking the door.

Maybe meeting here hadn't been such a good idea. But usually she had the place to herself, preferring to work at night. Her co-workers thought she worked late to impress the boss and resented her for it—as if she cared. But that was why meeting here had seemed ideal. No one ever came around at night and she didn't have to worry about her nosy old landlady eavesdropping.

"Who's there?" she called out, expecting an answer.

Silence.

She hadn't been afraid, hadn't had any reason to be afraid. Until now.

She heard Aunt Harriet snickering inside her head. "Told you this scheme would get you killed."

Nina hadn't considered how vulnerable she was, alone here in the plant. Dennison Ducks was ten miles from town and a good two miles from the nearest house, which was Wade Dennison's.

Another soft scuff of a shoe on the concrete. This one much closer. Her pulse jumped. Who was in the building with her? Someone who'd seen her car in the parking lot, known she was in here alone, maybe even knew exactly where she was in the building? Or one of the people she'd been expecting, only earlier? Either of them would have answered her. So who was in the building with her?

She could feel a presence on the other side of the row of ducks, someone moving slowly, purposefully, between the shelves toward her.

Panic filled her. She grabbed the duck off the table, smearing the wet paint. She could make a run for it around the opposite end of the shelves, dash for the door, but she knew it would be too easy for the person to cut her off before she got out—even if he didn't have a weapon.

She could hear breathing on the other side of the dense wall of carved ducks. It had to be someone who knew why she'd come to Timber Falls. Knew why she'd wanted to work at Dennison Ducks so badly. Someone who'd found out about her meeting here tonight. Someone who thought he could keep her from getting what she deserved. That narrowed it down considerably.

But which one was dumb enough to try to stop her? She thought she knew as she waited, clutching the large wooden duck in her fist, determined not to let anyone take what was rightfully hers. Not again.

She listened as the footsteps moved closer and closer—stopping at the end of the ceiling-high shelf filled with ducks nearest her.

Quietly she slipped to the end of the row and raised the duck over her head. *Come on. Just a few more steps...*

The figure came around the end of the wall of duck-filled shelves.

Nina stared in confusion. For an instant, she almost laughed she was so relieved. She lowered the duck. She had nothing to fear.

She couldn't have been more mistaken.

k Sissy Walker stood, hands on her ample hips,
of irritation on her face. He knew the look

Chapter Two

Wednesday, October 28

Early the next morning, an ill wind whirled through
Timber Falls. It started at the north end of Main,
down by the Ho Hum Motel. Just a breeze. But by
the time it reached Betty's Café, it had picked up
speed, dirt and dried leaves, stripping Lydia Abernathy's maple tree bare.

Now a dust devil, it reeled past the Spit Curl, the
post office and the *Timber Falls Courier,* discarding
leaves and dust like unwelcome offerings in each
doorway of the small Oregon town.

By the time the dust devil swept past Harry's
Hardware and the Duck-In bar, the sky was dark as
mud.

As if sensing more than an ill wind had blown into
town, Sheriff Mitch Tanner got up from his desk at
Town Hall to close the window moments before the
panes began to rattle. Dirt and debris clattered against
the glass. The dense wall of rain forest surrounding

town shimmered in the dull light, a flickering of dark shadows from within.

Just as suddenly as it had begun, the wind died, the dust and debris settled, leaves floated gently to the ground and the first drops of rain *plinked* against the window.

The rainy season in Timber Falls had begun.

Mitch groaned. Trouble always seemed to accompany the rain. And he feared, this year both had come early. To make matters worse, Halloween was only days away and he'd heard that the Duck-In bar was hosting a costume party. He could figure on a long night of breaking up fights and trying to get locals home safely.

Behind him, Wade Dennison cleared his throat. "As I was saying, Sheriff…"

Mitch dragged his gaze from the rain-streaked window, trying to shake an ominous sense of dread as he turned his attention back to the man sitting across the desk from him.

Over sixty, his dark hair peppered with gray, Wade Dennison had a look of privilege about him.

"It just isn't like Nina not to show for work." Wade was a soft-spoken man, but a powerful one in this town. He owned Dennison Ducks, Timber Falls's claim to fame—and its main source of income.

Mitch nodded, wondering why Wade was in such a tizzy. This couldn't be the first employee who hadn't shown up for work.

"I called. Her landlady said she didn't come home last night," Wade was saying.

"She doesn't have a cell phone?"

Wade shook his head, worry in his gaze.

was appropriate for a young and attractive female employee?

"Could be she stayed over at a friend's or a boyfriend's," Mitch suggested. "Or maybe she's with family."

Wade shook his head. "She doesn't have any family. No boyfriend, either. Or friends."

Mitch raised a brow.

"At least not that I know of," Wade added. "She's only been in town a month."

A month was plenty long enough to make friends, let alone a boyfriend. But Mitch didn't say anything.

Wade shifted in his chair. "Nina's…shy. Keeps to herself. She's real serious, you know?"

He didn't. But he was curious about how Wade knew all this. Mitch had seen Nina Monroe only a few times around town and just in passing, but he remembered her as being attractive with long dark hair and dark eyes. "Serious how?"

"She's a good worker, always on time," Wade was saying. "In fact, she works late a lot, real serious about her job." The older man cleared his throat again. "That's why I'm worried something might have happened to her."

Mitch's radar clicked on. "Like what?"

Wade shook his head. "I'm just saying she would have called if she wasn't coming in."

A shadow filled the open office doorway. Town

a look of [illegible] only too well.

"Ms. Jenkins on line two," she said. "It's the *fifth* time she's called this morning. She says if you don't talk to her, she'll track you down like a dog."

Mitch groaned, knowing that was no idle threat. "Wade, I have the information on Nina that you gave me. Let me do some checking and get back to you."

Wade Dennison slowly rose to his feet. "You'll let me know as soon as you hear something."

It wasn't a question. "You know I will." After Wade closed the office door behind him, Mitch picked up the phone and hit line two. "Charity?" It was never good news when Charity Jenkins called.

"Hello, Mitch," she said, a hint of humor in her tone. No doubt because she'd managed to get him on the line—in more ways than one over the years.

"You know threatening a sheriff is against the law," he said, always surprised by what just the sound of her voice did to him.

She laughed. She had a great laugh. "You gonna lock me up?" She made it sound like something she wouldn't mind.

He tried to imagine Charity in one of his cells and shook his head at even the thought. "What's so important that you've got Sissy ticked off already this morning?"

"Sissy is always ticked off," Charity said. "I called about the latest news."

He wasn't sure what news that might be. Knowing

Charity, she'd probably already gotten wind of Nina Monroe's alleged disappearance. The woman was a bloodhound.

Charity owned the local weekly, *Timber Falls Courier,* she'd started straight out of college, her journalism degree in her hot little hands. Mitch secretly believed she'd only started the newspaper as an excuse to butt into everyone's business—especially his. He was sure she couldn't make much money at it in a town the size of Timber Falls. But as he knew only too well, Charity loved a challenge.

"What news is that?" He hated to ask.

"Don't tell me you haven't heard! There's been a Bigfoot sighting on the edge of town. Frank, the Granny's bread deliveryman, saw it clear as day in his headlights last night. Practically ran off the road he was so upset."

Mitch swore under his breath. Bigfoot. Great. The news couldn't have been worse if an alien spaceship had landed at Dennison Ducks and abducted Nina Monroe. *Bigfoot.* This sort of thing only brought more wackos to town—as if Timber Falls needed that. And during the rainy season!

"I'm over at Betty's having breakfast," Charity said.

This was not anything new. He could imagine her sitting on her usual stool at the café. The sight was more than appealing. She'd be wearing jeans and a sweater that would hug her curves. Her burnished auburn hair would be pulled up into a ponytail. Or maybe down around her shoulders, falling in natural loose curls around her face, making her big brown eyes golden as summer sunshine.

"Everyone's talking about the sighting," she was saying. "I hear it's made all the big papers."

He groaned, hating to think how many people would drive up this way hoping to get a glimpse of the mythical creature. Just the way they did the last time. Damn.

"Betty made banana-cream pie," Charity said. She was making his mouth water and she knew it. The woman was relentless. "Have you had breakfast?"

Only Charity Jenkins would think pie was the "breakfast of champions." Not that he hadn't spent a good share of his mornings over the years on the stool next to her having pie for breakfast. The woman had corrupted him in ways he hated even to think about.

But not this morning. "As enticing as your offer is, I have to pass." Charity would do anything for a story, including tempt him with banana-cream pie. But he wasn't about to say something he would regret so she could print it.

Besides, he had to get on the Nina Monroe case, if there was a case, and the last thing he needed was to start the rainy season by spending time with Charity Jenkins. Hadn't he learned his lesson with that woman?

"Is there something going on I should know about?" she asked, always on alert.

"No," he said quickly. Probably too quickly. "I just don't want anything to do with this article. You

know how I feel about these damned Bigfoot sightings. Fools seeing things that we all know don't exist
and then shooting off their mouths.''

"Can I quote you on that?''

"No! And speaking of fools, make sure there is
no mention of my father and Bigfoot this time. I
mean it, Charity.''

She made a disgruntled sound. "You really are no
fun.''

"Yeah, so you keep telling me.'' She'd always
said he had no imagination because he didn't buy into
flying saucers, ghosts or marriage. If she hadn't already, she could add Bigfoot to that list.

"Well, all right, if you're sure. By the way,'' she
said in that seductive soft tone of hers, "thanks for
the present.''

"Present?''

"The one you left on my doorstep?'' She didn't
sound very sure.

"Charity, I didn't leave you a present.''

"Oh, I thought…''

He heard the disappointment in her voice. He hated
hurting her. It was one of the reasons he would never
have left her a present. "Sorry, it wasn't me.''

She let out a small sigh as if she should have
known. Just as she should have known not to set her
heart on marrying him. But she had, anyway.

Despite his feelings for her, he couldn't marry her.
Couldn't marry anyone. But especially Charity. Just
the thought of mixing their genes made him break
out in a cold sweat.

"I wonder who could have left the present, then?" she said more to herself than to him.

He wondered the same thing. Hadn't he known it was only a matter of time before some man swept Charity off her feet? Knowing it was one thing. Having it actually happen... It surprised him how much the idea of Charity with another man rattled him.

"I almost forgot," she said. "Didn't I just see Wade Dennison come out of your office a few minutes ago? Something going on at Dennison Ducks I should know about?"

This Charity he could deal with. "Not everything is a news story. Or any of your business."

Charity laughed. "We both know better than that."

He hung up and saw Sissy in the doorway again, giving him one of her why-don't-you-do-something-about-that-woman? looks. "Let me ask you something," he said before she could start to nag him about his personal life. "Do you think Wade Dennison is handsome?"

"Not my type."

"No, I mean, do women find him...attractive?"

She snorted. "He's got money, so hell yes, women find him attractive."

Mitch shook his head, wondering why it was so hard to get a straight answer out of a woman. "Is it possible that Wade and a twenty-something woman might—"

"I see where you're going with this," she interrupted impatiently. "Would he be interested in a woman young enough to be his daughter?'' Her brows shot up. ''Wade Dennison is a man, isn't he?'' With that she turned and marched back to her desk.

Mitch shook his head and looked at the information Wade had given him. But his thoughts veered off again to Charity and the ''present'' some secret admirer had left her. It bothered him that the man didn't have the guts to come forward and make his intentions known. He wondered who the guy was. And what his intentions were.

With a curse, he again looked at what Wade had given him, focusing on Nina Monroe's address. He groaned when he saw who her landlady was—Charity's Aunt Florie. This town was too damned small, and it only seemed to get smaller when the rainy season began.

CHARITY JENKINS took a bite of the banana-cream pie, closed her eyes and instantly conjured up the image of Mitch Tanner. Something about the combination of sugar, cream and butter...

Of course, she'd been thinking about Mitch since she was four, so it came pretty easy after twenty-two years.

It was odd, though, the way she saw him in her daydreams. If she was eating something rich and wonderful, like banana-cream pie, then Mitch always appeared in snug-fitting worn jeans and a T-shirt that accentuated his broad muscled chest and shoulders. Without fail, he would be smiling at her, the sunlight on his tanned face, his eyes as blue as the Pacific.

Other foods, however, such as vegetables or any-thing low-fat, had Mitch in his sheriff's uniform, scowling at her in disapproval. For obvious reasons, she avoided those foods.

She took another bite of pie, closed her eyes and was startled when Mitch popped up in her daydream wearing a black tuxedo and standing at an altar.

Her eyes flew open, her heart pounding. *Her* wedding? The one she'd imagined and planned since age four?

On this, she was not mistaken. Mitch in a black tux, she in white satin. Or maybe white silk. Or lace. The imagined wedding changed, depending on her mood. But the groom never had.

"The pie all right?" Betty asked as she stopped on the other side of the counter.

"De-e-elicious," Charity said, closing her eyes again and licking her lips in true delight, hoping to see Mitch in that wedding tux again. No such luck. She opened her eyes as Betty refilled her diet cola.

Betty Garrett was a pleasingly plump bottled-blond on this side of fifty but who could pass for thirty-five in a pinch and had a talent for attracting the wrong men the way a white blouse attracts blackberry jam. She'd married and changed her last name so many times that most people in town couldn't tell you what it was at any given moment. Right now Betty was between men, but it wouldn't last long. It never did.

"I just put a couple of lemon-meringue pies in the oven in case you're interested," Betty said.

Interested? Lemon meringue was her second favorite.

"I figure this Bigfoot sighting will bring 'em in for sure. Did last time," the older woman said. "I decided I'd better make some extra pies."

Bigfoot sightings packed the town. The curious drove up to Timber Falls in hopes of seeing what some called the Hill Ghost or Sasquatch.

"I heard the No Vacancy sign is already on at the Ho Hum and a half-dozen campers are parked over by the old train depot," Betty was saying. Everyone wanted to see Bigfoot and prove the legendary creature's existence.

None as badly as Charity Jenkins, though. Every journalist dreamed of that one big story. The Pulitzer-prize winner. Charity yearned to write about something other than church dinners and wooden decoys. The truth was, she desperately needed one big story. It was the only way she could make everyone in this town see that she wasn't like the rest of her family, she was a normal level-headed woman and a serious journalist. All right, she didn't care about everyone in town. She just wanted to prove it to Mitch.

She took the last bite of her pie, savoring it, eyes closed. No Mitch in jeans or a tux. She opened her eyes, disappointed.

"Where do you put it all?" Betty asked with a shake of her head as she took the empty plate.

Charity was blessed. Probably because she was a fidgeter. She couldn't sit still. Nor did she ever stop thinking. Like right now. Between planning how to play the Bigfoot sighting in tomorrow's paper, she was thinking about Mitch and if her banana-cream-pie fantasy had any credibility.

Just the thought of Mitch standing next to her at the altar was enough to burn up a whole day's worth of calories. She and Mitch had a history, an off-and-on-again attachment that went as far back as shared glue in kindergarten.

Right now they were at a slight lull in their relationship: he pretended he was a confirmed bachelor and she pretended she was going to let him stay that way.

This morning she'd been so excited when she'd seen the present on her doorstep. She'd been so sure it was from Mitch. Who else? But he'd sworn it hadn't been him. And why pretend he hadn't left it if he had? Then again, why pretend he wasn't wild about her when he obviously was? She'd never understand the man.

"Would you look at this place?" Betty said, shaking her head. The café was full, everyone talking about the Bigfoot sighting. "I can't believe these fools are still arguing over Bigfoot after all these years."

Charity glanced around the small café. It was the only place in town to sit down and eat, plus it was *the* place to get homemade pies and cinnamon rolls and the latest scuttlebutt.

As she picked up her diet cola, she had an eerie feeling that someone was watching her. It wasn't the first time, either. She turned and caught a flash of black on the street outside. Her breath caught as a black pickup drove by. It was the same black truck she'd seen last night by her house and again on her way to Betty's this morning. Both times she'd had the feeling the driver was watching her.

She shivered as she watched the truck disappear up Main Street. While she could only make out a large shape behind the dark-tinted windows, she could feel the driver watching her through the rain. Her stomach tightened, remembering the present she'd found on her doorstep this morning. Could one have anything to do with the other?

RAIN HAMMERED the roof of the Sheriff's Department patrol car, mist rising ghostlike from the drenched pavement, as Mitch drove out to the address Wade had given him for Nina Monroe. A swollen gray sky hung low over the pines as if closing in the tiny town, limiting more than visibility.

Mitch dreaded another rainy season in Timber Falls, especially one that appeared to be starting a month early and could last until at least April. It wasn't just the endless rain or the dull overcast days. Without fail, the rainy season seemed to bring out the worst in the residents.

One year, Bud Harper hung himself from a beam in his garage just days before the sun shone. Another year, a local guy shot up the Duck-In bar when he caught his wife there with another man. And twenty-seven years ago, during the worst rainy season of all,

Wade and Daisy Dennison's baby girl Angela disappeared from her crib, never to be found.

It was always during the rainy season that strange and often horrible things happened in this small isolated town deep in the Cascades. It was as if the gloomy days, when the rain never stopped, did something to make the residents behave more oddly than usual. As if on those days, the only place to look was inward. And sometimes that was as dark as the day—and far more disturbing.

And if the rain wasn't bad enough, there was the forest that surrounded Timber Falls, imprisoned it, really, and constantly had to be fought back as if it was at war with the tiny town. As he drove past the city limits, the forest formed almost a canopy over the two-lane highway, a tunnel of green darkness over the only road out.

To the clack of the wipers, he turned off in front of a cottage-style house with a dozen smaller bungalows lined up behind it. Years ago, the place had been a motel. But not long after Wade Dennison started his decoy factory, Florence Jenkins had taken down the motel sign and started renting out the bungalows as apartments.

It was about the same time that Florence discovered her hidden powers. The sign out front now read: Madam Florie's. Under it was her Web site address.

Nina Monroe had been renting from Charity's Aunt Florie, Timber Falls's self-proclaimed clairvoyant.

Mitch braced himself then climbed out of his patrol car and hurried through the pouring rain to the front door.

When an elderly woman opened the door, he tipped his hat, dreading this more than he'd imagined. "Mornin', Florie."

"Sheriff. I've been expecting you." She smiled knowingly, her eyes twinkling in her lined face. "Saw that you'd be by in my coffee dregs this morning."

He nodded. If Florie could see the future in her coffee cup, more power to her. He just didn't want to hear about his own future. He wanted to be surprised.

She motioned him in with a dramatic sweep of her arm, reminding him of some exotic, brightly feathered bird. Florie was sixty if she was a day. Her dyed flame-red hair swirled around her head like a turban. She wore a flamboyant caftan, large gold hoop earrings, several dozen jangling bracelets and a thick layer of turquoise eye shadow.

Florie and her much younger sister Fredricka, Charity's mother, had been raised by hippies in a commune just outside of town. Freddie still lived on the old commune property with a dozen other people but seldom came into town. While Freddie raised organic vegetables, Florie predicted the future to tourists in the summer and locals during the rainy season—another reason Mitch had cause for concern during the rainy season.

The old motel office was painted black and had recessed lighting that illuminated the only piece of

furniture in the room—a purple-velvet-covered table
with a crystal ball at its center. Florie had had the
ball shipped in from a store in Portland. It gleamed
darkly, as if mirroring the weather outside.

"I suppose your coffee dregs also told you *why*
I'm here," he said as he entered. "Or maybe Wade
mentioned it when he called you about Nina Monroe
not showing up for work?"

Florie gave him an annoyed look and pointed to a
sign on the wall in the entry that read No Negative
Thoughts. A series of other small signs advertised
palm, tarot and crystal ball readings.

"I was concerned after what I saw in my cup this
morning," she said, lifting one tweezed dyed-red
brow as she waited for him to ask.

No way was he going there.

"It involved my niece Charity," she added, not a
woman to give up easily, a trait she shared with her
niece.

"I understand that Nina Monroe rents from you
and she didn't come home last night," he said, cutting to the chase.

Florie nodded, obviously disappointed by his lack
of curiosity about those telltale coffee dregs.

"How do you know she didn't come home last
night and then leave again before you got up?" he
asked.

"Because I was up until daylight." At his surprised look, she added, "My Internet business—
horoscopes, tarot cards, psychic readings, all by

e-mail. You really should get your chart done. I'm concerned about your aura.''

He had worse things to worry about than his aura right now. "I need to see Nina's bungalow."

Florie stepped behind a dark-velvet curtain. She came back with a key attached to a round small cardboard tag.

When he reached for the key, she took his hand and turned it palm up.

"Ah, a long life line with a single marriage." She beamed and dropped the key into his palm.

He shook his head. His palm lied. His parents' marriage had more than convinced him what his future *didn't* hold—a wedding.

"'Aries'?" he asked, reading the lettering on the key's tag.

"I try to match my guests and their bungalows based on their horoscopes. Better karma."

"So Nina was an Aries?"

"No, the Aries bungalow just happened to be the only unit I had open when she showed up."

He reminded himself that Charity shared Florie's genes. All the more reason to keep Charity at arm's length. Several car lengths would be even better. "So what was Nina?"

Florie shrugged. "She wouldn't tell me her birth sign. Can you believe some people aren't interested in enlightenment?"

He could. "Nina rented the bungalow in September?"

"Drove up in that little red compact of hers looking for a room. September nineteenth. I remember because she didn't even have a job yet. But that very afternoon, she got one at Dennison Ducks. Kismet, I guess.''

Or something like that. "No need for you to come out in the rain with me.''

Florie took a bright purple raincoat from the closet and a pair of matching purple galoshes. "I wouldn't dream of letting you go alone. I've been picking up some really weird vibes from that girl,'' she said, and stepped past him and out the front door.

He followed her around back through the rain to the first of twelve bungalows, the one with the Aries symbol on the door.

Standing on the small porch, he felt a sudden chill as if someone had walked over his grave. Florie knocked, then cautiously unlocked the door.

"Oh, my!'' she cried as the door swung open on the ransacked bungalow.

"Stay here,'' he ordered, and stepped inside to look for Nina Monroe's body in the mess.

Chapter Three

"You all right?" Betty asked, looking concerned.

Charity turned back to the counter as the black pickup disappeared from view in the steady torrent of rain. "I just thought I saw..." She shook her head, catching herself. "Nothing."

She didn't want it all over town that she thought somebody in a black pickup was following her. Or that she'd found a present on her doorstep, a palm-size heart-shaped red stone in a small white box with a bright-red ribbon and a small card that read THINK-ING OF YOU in computer-generated letters. No name.

"Is it me or is the whole town on edge today?" Betty said. "Kind of gives you the creeps thinking that Frank might really have seen Bigfoot."

"Yeah." Charity turned again to look through the rain to the dense forest beyond the street. The foliage was so thick that not even light could get through in places. Who knew what lived there?

Charity shivered. "Frank's a pretty reliable witness," she said. "He saw *some*thing. Something he thought was Bigfoot, at least."

Betty nodded and moved away. Behind Charity, several other diners began arguing amongst themselves.

"All Frank saw was a bear," said one.

"A bear that walks on its hind legs?" said another.

"It was dark," a third put in. "Probably just saw a shadow move across the road."

"I say it's some ancient ancestor. You know, a former race of giants."

"Who just happens to live in the Timber Falls mountains and never comes out? Puh-leeze."

Charity had heard these arguments for years.

She went back to thinking about Mitch. No hardship there. She'd so hoped he'd left the present. Just as she hoped he'd change his mind about marriage. She knew he wanted her, but just not on her terms. If she'd settle for anything else…

Well, she wouldn't. Couldn't. No matter how tempted she was. She was the one in the family who was going to do it the right way, not like her mother, who had three daughters—Faith, Hope and, what else, Charity—and hadn't bothered to get married until all three were old enough to be bridesmaids.

It was embarrassing to come from a family of not just old hippies but screwballs. Was it any wonder Mitch was scared to death to marry her and have children, given her genes?

That was why she had to show him. He'd been surprised when she'd gotten her journalism degree and started her own newspaper. Now all she needed was a Pulitzer-prize-winning story. She would change the family's image, even if it killed her, by doing everything the way it should be—right down to the wedding in white.

"Charity, tell them," Betty called to her from across the café. "Tell them about all those Bigfoot sightings going years back and all over the world."

"It's true," Charity said, pulling herself away from her daydream. "A creature like Bigfoot has been reported in every state except Hawaii and Rhode Island. More than two hundred sightings going back to ancient man and probably untold numbers of people who have seen something and kept it to themselves because they were afraid of being ridiculed."

"Yeah, then how come no one's ever found any Bigfoot bones?" another customer asked.

"Maybe they bury their dead," someone replied.

"Or the bodies decay too quickly in this kind of climate," someone else suggested.

"Or Bigfoot is nothing but a myth," still another said.

"Charity, you really believe Bigfoot exists, don't you?" Betty asked as she refilled her diet cola.

A woman who hung on to the belief that one day she'd get Mitch Tanner to marry her? Oh, yeah. "He not only exists, but one of these days I'm going to prove it."

"You do that!" Betty said, and shot an indignant look at the customers who laughed.

Charity could just imagine a photo of Bigfoot on the front page of her paper. Imagine the look on Mitch's face. He'd have to take her paper seriously then, wouldn't he? And her, as well.

But he'd also have to apologize to his father. Lee Tanner had become the laughingstock of Timber Falls a few years ago when he'd stumbled across a Bigfoot on his way home from the bar—and reported it. No one had taken him seriously because he'd been drunk. But Charity had seen the truth in his eyes. Lee had seen *some*thing out there that night. Something that scared the hell out of him.

"A confirmed Bigfoot sighting could really put Timber Falls on the map," said Twila Langsley.

Twila had put Timber Falls on the map six years back when Charity and Mitch had discovered some of Archibald Montgomery's mummified remains in the huge carpetbag Twila carried, the rest of him in a trunk at the end of her bed.

Archibald had been Twila's beau, and she, it seemed, had killed him more than fifty-odd years ago to keep him from running off with her best friend, Lorinda Nichols. Archie, the slick devil, had been romancing them both.

Twila did five years at the state pen. She got out on good behavior in time to celebrate her ninetieth birthday.

No one in town felt any ill will toward her. She just wasn't allowed to bring her old carpetbag into Betty's—even if all she carried in it now was her knitting.

"I don't think even Bigfoot could put Timber Falls on the map," Betty said.

"If there is a Bigfoot, it's got to be smart," one of the customers noted. "Smart enough to know we'd cage it or kill it if it came near us."

Betty laughed. "Smarter than my ex-husbands, then."

Charity thought about having another piece of pie, unable to get the image of Mitch Tanner in the tux out of her mind. Did she dare hope it meant what she thought it did?

She finished her soda and had started to leave when she saw the black pickup again. Her heart lodged in her throat as the pickup slowed. She could see the shadow of someone behind the tinted glass just before the driver sped away. One thing was certain. Whoever was driving that truck *was* following her.

"DID YOU FIND HER?" Florie asked from the doorway of the ransacked Aries bungalow.

Mitch shook his head. He didn't find a body, but he feared Wade was right about Nina Monroe's being in trouble.

"I told you I was picking up weird vibes," Florie said.

Mitch was picking up more than a few of his own.

The bungalow was tiny, just a living area, bedroom, bath and kitchenette, all furnished with garage-sale finds.

In the bedroom at the back sat a sagging double bed and a scarred chest of drawers beside an open closet door. The bath had a metal shower, sink and toilet. No storage.

It was obvious someone had searched the place, looking for something that was small enough to conceal under a couch cushion. Or in a toilet tank. Or at the back of a drawer. Drugs? It was Mitch's first thought.

"Any idea what they might have been looking for?" he asked Florie on the off chance she'd done more than pick up bad vibes.

She shook her head. "The girl didn't have much. I don't even think she owned a suitcase. The day she checked in here all she had was that old compact car and whatever she had stuffed into a large worn backpack."

He glanced through the open door of the bedroom. A stained and frayed navy nylon backpack lay on the floor, open and empty. "She talk to you about where she was from?"

"Didn't talk at all. I barely saw her. Got up early and came in late."

"Any friends stop by?" He knew Florie kept a pretty good eye on the comings and goings of her tenants. The crystal-ball business was fairly slow in a town the size of Timber Falls.

"There was a guy. A couple of nights ago."

Mitch's ears perked up. "What did he look like?"

"Didn't get a good look at him. It was too dark. She never used her porch light. But he was tall as you, wore dark clothing. I got the impression he didn't want to be seen."

"What did he drive?"

Again Florie shook her head. "He must have parked down the road," she said. "But they had one heck of a fight."

"About what?"

"That, I can't tell you. I could just hear the raised voices for a few moments, then nothing."

"You didn't recognize the man's voice?"

"That darn Kinsey had her stereo on too loud in the Aquarius bungalow next door," Florie said. "You know she's gone and dyed her hair cotton-candy pink. Like I'm going to let someone with pink hair cut my hair."

He nodded. Kinsey had come back from beautician school determined to make her mother's shop, the Spit Curl, hip.

Mitch moved to the bedroom, wondering who the man was Nina had been arguing with. Florie stayed in the bungalow doorway. Only a few items of clothing hung in the closet. Probably just what had fit into the backpack. Either Nina couldn't afford more or she hadn't brought all her belongings to Timber Falls.

A bell jangled outside. "It's my private line," Florie announced. "I'm going to have to take it. One of my clients needs me."

He could tell she hated to leave. This was probably the most excitement she'd had in years. But money was money. "I'll be here."

She nodded as the bell jangled again, then took off hunkered deep in her coat against the rain.

Mitch looked around the room, hoping to find an address book or some clue where Nina might be.

The room was bare except for the bed and four-drawer dresser. There were no knickknacks, no photos, no personal items other than clothing in here or in the living room.

All of the drawers in the dresser had been pulled

out, the sparse contents dumped on the floor. All except the bottom drawer.

He moved to the dresser, squatted down and pulled on the stuck drawer. Empty. Still squatting, he glanced under the bed. Nothing but dust balls.

The lack of clothing bothered him. Even counting what Nina was last seen wearing, the woman had only about four days' worth of clothes.

That seemed odd to him. But if there were more belongings, where were they? And why did she leave them behind when she'd come to Timber Falls?

It made him wonder if this was only to be a short stay.

He started to get up, shoving the drawer back in as he rose. It stuck. He had to pull hard to get the drawer to slide out again. As he did, he heard a soft metallic clink.

Withdrawing the drawer completely, he turned it over, curious what had made the sound. There were several pieces of torn masking tape stuck to the bottom. Something had been taped there but had broken loose.

Setting the drawer aside, he crouched down and felt around under the dresser until his fingers touched something small, metallic and cold.

His heart leaped as he withdrew a tarnished-silver baby's spoon and saw that the handle was in the shape of a duck's head. The same shape that had made Dennison Ducks famous. Even through the tarnish, he could read the name engraved on the spoon's handle: Angela. He felt a chill spike up his spine.

He'd heard that Wade Dennison had hired a jeweler in Eugene to make specially designed silverware for each of his daughters. First for Desiree, then two years later for Angela. Could this be Angela Dennison's baby spoon? And if it was, what was Nina doing with it twenty-seven years after the baby had disappeared from her crib?

CHARITY RAN through the rain to her old VW bug parked in front of Betty's and sat for a moment with the heater running as she tried to shake off her chill.

She'd seen the black truck again and there was no doubt in her mind that it was following her. Worse, she thought, looking at the small white box with the bright red ribbon sitting on her passenger seat, she suspected the driver had left her the present.

She stared at the box for a long moment before picking it up. There was no writing on it, not even a store logo. She opened the lid again and parted the white tissue paper.

Earlier all that had registered was that the stone was heart-shaped. She'd been so excited about getting a present from Mitch that she hadn't noticed that the stone was also blood-red and cold to the touch. She shivered as she turned the stone over.

There was nothing on it. No lettering. No artist's imprint. Nothing. The shiny surface seemed to capture what little light the gloomy day afforded, absorbing it deep within, as if harboring it like a secret.

She pulled out the tissue paper to make sure there wasn't something inside the box that she'd missed. Like a clue as to who had left it for her. Earlier it had seemed like a gift. Now it felt more like a threat.

She stuffed the heart back into the box, hurriedly closing the lid. The defroster had finally cleared enough of her windshield that she could drive the two blocks to the post office. But as she started to pull out, she caught a glimpse of a black pickup one street over.

She shifted into gear and took off after it. As she reached the corner, she half expected the truck to be gone. But there it was, creeping along as if the driver was lost. Or sightseeing. Could she be wrong about it following her?

There was only one way to find out, she thought, as she floored the gas, roared past the pickup and then hit her brakes, skidding sideways to block the street.

She leaped from her car into the pouring rain, ran up to the driver's side of the pickup and jerked the door open.

A startled gray-haired man stared out at her. Beside him, a younger woman with blond hair clasped both hands over her chest as if she was having a heart attack.

Too late Charity noticed that the windows on the pickup weren't tinted. This wasn't the black truck she'd seen earlier, the one she was sure had been following her. On closer inspection this pickup was a much newer model. Worse, she knew the driver.

"Charity?" the elderly man gasped.

She groaned. "Mr. Sawyer, I'm so sorry. I thought you were someone else." He'd left Timber Falls about ten years ago after his wife died, but he'd kept the old Victorian house at the edge of town that had been in his family for generations.

"What in heaven's name were you thinking?" the blonde next to him demanded.

"It's all right, Emily," Liam said to the woman. "It's just Charity Jenkins. She's a good friend of my daughter Roz's." He turned to Charity. "This is my wife, Emily. I've moved back home."

He'd remarried? And come back to Timber Falls? Charity had noticed someone painting the old place just the other day, but never dreamed Liam Sawyer would return.

"Congratulations," she said, trying to hide her surprise and embarrassment. "I hope that means Rozalyn will be coming up to visit." She hadn't seen her friend for several years now.

Liam smiled ruefully. "She's awfully busy. You know she's a famous photographer now."

Charity nodded, the rain dripping off the front of her hood. "I have all her books."

"Could we get going?" Emily asked Liam.

"I'm sorry," Charity said again, realizing the rain was getting into the pickup. Liam seemed oblivious to it, though. "I'll move my car."

He smiled at her. "It is good to see you, Charity. Please stop by and visit."

"Tell her to wait until we get settled," Emily said. "The place is a disaster. It's going to take months to get it into any shape at all."

Charity sprinted back to her car and hurriedly pulled away, thinking about Roz as she drove to the post office to pick up her mail. She and Roz had been inseparable as kids. Of course Roz would be coming to visit her father, no matter how busy she was. It would be good to see her again.

Postmistress Sarah Bridges looked up as Charity came into the small post office. "Just got all the mail out," Sarah said from behind the caged opening on the left. To the right was a row of mailboxes.

"Anything good in mine?" Charity asked as she walked down to her box and, using her key, opened it to see a stack of bills.

"You know I never pay any attention to who gets what," Sarah called from behind the wall of boxes.

Uh-huh. Charity flipped through the stack as she walked back to where Sarah stood. Sarah was a good source of gossip.

"So what's new?" she asked Sarah.

"Liam Sawyer's remarried and back in town."

Darn. Charity hoped she had the jump on that story. No such luck. "I know. I just saw them."

Sarah shot her a look. "What do you think of the new wife?"

Charity might have shared her thoughts on Emily Sawyer if it hadn't been for an old loyalty to Roz. "I only saw her for a minute."

Sarah nodded, lips pursed, eyeing her as if she was holding out. "Well, you have a good day."

Charity doubted that, given how the day had gone so far. She pushed open the door and made a run for her car through the rain. She hadn't gone but a few steps when she caught a movement from the alley between the post office and bank.

An instant later she was hit by what felt like a

freight train. Her mail went flying as she was knocked down in the mud by someone wearing a large dark raincoat. The cloaked figure stopped, back turned to her and knelt to hurriedly scoop up her mail from the wet ground.

She pushed herself up into a sitting position, too stunned to stand—until she realized the person in the dark raincoat wasn't picking up her mail to give her, but going through it!

"Hey!" Charity cried.

The dark raincoat didn't turn. Behind her Charity heard Sarah come out of the post office. "Charity?"

The figure dropped the mail and took off at a run down the alley.

"What in the world?" Sarah demanded, charging out to scoop up the wet mail and help Charity to her feet as the dark raincoat disappeared around the corner.

Charity took the mail from Sarah, her gaze still on the street where the figure had vanished. She heard an engine start in the distance. A few seconds later, a black pickup with tinted windows roared off two blocks away.

MITCH TUCKED the baby spoon in his pocket as Florie swept back into the bungalow on a gust of wind and rain.

"How's the client?" he asked, trying to cover the fact that she'd startled him.

"Problems of the heart," she said with a wave of her hand. "She's going to call me back. Have you figured out where Nina has gone?"

He shook his head. "When she arrived she didn't have a job, you said."

Florie nodded. "She asked me about a bungalow, I said I had one, she said she'd take it and then she asked me how to get to Dennison Ducks."

So Nina had been confident she was going to get a job at the decoy plant. It *was* the biggest business in town, and maybe Nina had experience that made her confident she'd be hired. But Mitch also knew jobs at the plant were hard to come by. Nor were there many openings, because wages and benefits were good and with so few jobs in Timber Falls, employees tended to stay.

"What kind of paperwork did you get her to fill out before you rented her the bungalow?" Mitch asked, hoping for a clue as to Nina Monroe's life before she showed up here.

"None, other than her name," Florie said with a shake of her head. "I just go by whatever vibe I pick up."

"Vibes, instead of a former address or references?" he asked, unable to hide his disbelief.

"I'll have you know vibes are much more reliable than references."

He sighed. "But you told me her vibes were bad."

Florie flushed. "Actually, no, I said they were weird. I remember thinking she was awfully nervous. From her aura I could tell she had man trouble. But with women that's usually the case, isn't it?"

"But you rented to her, anyway?"

"She had cash," Florie said with an embarrassed shrug.

He counted to ten. "She get any phone calls while she was here?"

"Just one. From some woman. Sounded old. Maybe her mother, or grandmother. Nina didn't want to the take the call but finally did. I heard a little of it. Nina said, 'How did you find me? I told you to leave me alone.' She paused, then said, 'Right, you're worried about me. That's a laugh. Don't call here again. You're just going to mess things up.'"

Not bad for hearing only a "little" of a one-sided conversation. "The woman ever call again?"

Florie shook her head. "And before you ask, the number was blocked. You know, on my caller ID. I only checked because I didn't like the vibes I got from the caller. Just like what I'm picking up now about Nina. Worse vibes than before, you know?"

He knew, thinking of the missing woman and the baby spoon in his pocket.

Chapter Four

Back at his office, Mitch closed the door and went straight to his computer. He typed in Nina Monroe's name and her social security number Wade had given him—not surprised by the results.

Nina Monroe had lied about not only her social security number, but her name, as well.

"I'm going to get some doughnuts," Sissy said, sticking her head in the door.

"Lemon-filled?"

She nodded and smiled. "You need anything before I go?"

He shook his head and waited until he heard her leave before he went down to the basement where the old files were kept.

He dug out Angela Dennison's file, dusted it off and took it back upstairs.

Sheriff Bill "Hud" Hudson had been like a father to Mitch, as well as a mentor and friend. Hud had also been a first-rate sheriff and the reason Mitch had taken the same career path, instead of following his father's example and becoming a drunk.

Hud had been sheriff at the time of Angela's disappearance. At first, it was believed that the baby had been kidnapped. But no ransom demand was ever made and no body was ever found.

Not far into the file, Mitch started seeing a pattern, one he didn't like. In these types of cases, the parents are usually the first suspects, and Wade and Daisy Dennison were no exceptions.

In Sheriff Hudson's interview with Daisy, she testified that she didn't recall seeing Wade until the baby was discovered missing the next morning. She'd said she'd gone to bed early and didn't know when Wade had gotten home.

Wade, however, said he returned home at his usual time to find that Daisy had been drinking. They'd argued. She'd gone to bed. He'd slept in the den until he was wakened by the nanny early the next morning screaming that the baby was gone.

The nanny, Alma Bromdale, said she'd put the baby to bed about eight that night and gone to bed early herself. She'd taken some cold medicine that made her drowsy and thought that was why she hadn't heard anything in the adjacent room where the baby was sleeping.

That meant none of the three had an alibi.

Alma Bromdale. Mitch wrote down the name in his notebook. The nanny had been with the Dennisons for more than two years. She'd been hired just before the Dennisons first daughter, Desiree, was born. Alma was twenty-five at the time, from Coos Bay and had listed her job experience as one previous nanny job, baby-sitting and a nanny course through the adult-education program at the high school. She must be about fifty-two now.

Alma had been fired the day after the presumed kidnapping and had left Timber Falls. Mitch checked the telephone directory online. There was only one Bromdale in Coos Bay—Harriet Bromdale. A relative? He wrote down that name, as well, wondering what in the hell he was doing.

So he found an old baby's spoon with a Dennison duck head and ''Angela'' engraved on it. And so Nina Monroe was the right age and was now missing. Did he really think Nina might be the missing Angela?

He looked down at the file again, shaking his head. He didn't know what to think. Hud had noted in his interview with Alma that she'd seemed scared and upset, both natural for someone who'd just learned that the baby she was responsible for had been stolen—and from the adjacent room.

Alma had admitted that Wade and Daisy fought and, yes, she'd overheard them arguing about the paternity of the baby. Wade didn't think it was his.

Mitch swore under his breath.

The alleged kidnapper had climbed the trellis to the second-story room, but was believed to have taken the baby down the back stairs and out through a rear door on the first floor. Unfortunately, Sheriff Hudson had noted Wade had initiated a search of the area, using a few Dennison Duck employees, before calling the sheriff, and they'd tracked all over and destroyed any evidence there might have been outside the baby's bedroom window.

Baby Angela had been wearing a pink nightshirt. The only other item taken from the room was the quilt from her bed. Nothing else. No baby spoon, but Mitch knew that the spoon could have easily been overlooked.

He continued down the list of suspects to the live-in housekeeper who'd been fired a week before the abduction, a woman by the name of Georgette Bonners.

Georgette had been angry and, like Alma, had nothing good to say about the Dennisons. She had also alluded to the fighting and the question of the baby's paternity.

On the night of the abduction, Georgette said she was with her husband, Tim. He confirmed it. Both were now deceased.

Mitch closed the file, telling himself he was probably barking up the wrong tree. But there was that damned spoon. And Nina Monroe was missing. He put the file in his drawer and locked it.

As Sissy came in with the doughnuts, he grabbed his coat and headed for the door, taking the lemon-filled doughnut she shoved at him on his way out with a grin and a thanks.

The road to Dennison Ducks was narrow and dark, ten miles carved through the forest. Today, with the rain beating down, the road was even darker, gloomy somehow.

Or maybe it was just his mood, which hadn't been helped by the thought of that damned present someone had left for Charity. She'd sounded so excited. He wondered now what the gift had been.

Dennison Ducks was Timber Falls's claim to fame. Of course, if Wade Dennison had his way, the town would be renamed Dennison. Or even Dennison Ducks. Fortunately Wade didn't have his way *all* the time.

The decoys were sold in a small outlet store in town next to the *Timber Falls Courier* office, from mid-April to mid-October. But few people knew where the ducks were actually carved, since none were sold on site at the plant. There wasn't even a Dennison Ducks sign on the large metal building, just a small sign at the gravel parking lot that read Employees Only.

There was no gate. No security guard. And since no one lived on the premises, no one had seen Nina Monroe arrive or leave last night, according to Wade.

This morning there were a half-dozen cars in the lot. Mitch had called on the way to make sure Wade was in his office. He was and had told Mitch he could talk to any of the workers he needed to. Earlier Mitch had suspected Wade hadn't been telling him everything. Now, after seeing Nina's ransacked bungalow, he was convinced of it. He parked and rang the bell at the employee entrance. The door was opened by Bud Farnsworth, the production manager.

Mitch was assaulted by the heavy scent of freshly cut pine as he entered the building. From deep inside came the drone of band saws, carving machines and sanders. Ducks in various stages of production lined the tall metal shelves that ran the length of the room.

"Wade said you'd be coming by." Bud didn't sound happy about that. "You know this is our busiest time of the year, gearing up for Christmas." He was a burly fifty-something man with receding dark hair and small dark eyes that always seemed to be squinted in a frown. Like most of the employees, he'd started working at the decoy plant in high school and had worked his way up.

Bud drank on his time off and it showed in his ruddy complexion, as well as in his cranky demeanor, probably the result of a hangover. "Before you bother to ask, I don't know anything about Nina Monroe. She didn't work for me. Never said two words to her." Bud's crankiness verged on hostility. "Paint department's down there." He pointed between the shelves of ducks.

"If you think of anything that might help, give me a call," Mitch said to the man's retreating back.

Bud gave no sign he'd heard.

Mitch rounded the end of the last shelf to what was obviously the paint department. Three artists were seated at a large wooden table next to a window. Both the table and the floor around them were covered in dried paint. One of the four chairs at the table was empty. Nina Monroe's.

Mitch made his way to the painters, recognizing all three women. The thing about living in a small town like Timber Falls was that everyone knows everyone else—and their business. For most people, that was a curse. For the town sheriff, it was a mixed blessing.

Sheryl Bends didn't look up as he dragged out the empty chair next to her and sat down. He'd gone to school with Sheryl, even kissed her once in junior high. She was divorced from Fred Bends, a local logger, had worked at Dennison Ducks since high school and spent most evenings at the Duck-In Bar.

She had a narrow face with strong features and wide pale-green eyes, and wore her brown hair in a single braid that fell to the middle of her back. She often invited him over for dinner at her place. He'd never accepted, although he'd been tempted on occasion—usually when he just couldn't get Charity off his mind. But he'd never been tempted·enough to actually accept.

Sheryl wore her usual outfit—a Western shirt, jeans, moccasins and long beaded earrings. Both the shirt and jeans seemed to be fighting to keep her ample breasts and bottom from bursting out.

"Hello, Sheriff," Sheryl said, giving him one of her slow sexy smiles.

"Sheryl." He felt his face warm a little.

From across the table, Tracy Shank seemed amused to see him flustered. Tracy was thirty-something with cropped brown hair and close-set eyes. She gave him a nod and kept working.

Next to her sat Pat Ames. She was fiftyish with a head of gray curly hair and a small delicate frame.

"Sheriff," Pat said, and kept painting the drake decoy in front of her.

He turned his attention to Nina's workspace, hoping to find some personal item that might give him a clue as to her whereabouts. But while the other women had photos of husbands or boyfriends or kids, there was nothing personal at Nina's end.

Mitch watched the women work for a moment, wondering if he should talk to them separately. He hoped they'd be more honest as a group. Also, he was still expecting Nina to turn up. It wasn't as if he had a murder investigation on his hands.

"I suppose you heard I'm looking for Nina Monroe."

They had. He went through his questions with Pat and Tracy, who told him what they knew, with Sheryl nodding in agreement. According to the women, Nina stayed to herself, didn't talk much, didn't socialize with her fellow workers, didn't even eat her brown-bag lunch with them.

"Where'd she eat lunch?" he asked, having noticed what looked like a coffee-break room on his way in.

The women shrugged. "She'd leave the building,"

Pat said quietly as she carefully painted a patch of Mallard green on her duck decoy.

"She ate outside?" he asked.

Pat shrugged and whispered, "Wade usually left for lunch right after her." Pat didn't look at him, just kept working.

"You think there was something going on between them?" he asked, keeping his voice down, too.

No answer.

Sheryl glanced past his shoulder. He followed her gaze to the large plate-glass window of Wade's office on the second floor. The office was situated so that it overlooked the plant floor, giving him a view of the entire production area. Wade stood at the window, watching.

Mitch shoved back his chair, stood and thanked the women before heading upstairs.

Wade was still standing at the glass looking down when Mitch stepped into his office. He turned, not looking happy. But then, he seldom did.

"Have you found out anything?" he demanded.

"Not much. I'd like to see Nina's employment file."

"I don't know what help it'll be." Wade motioned for Mitch to draw up a chair in front of his desk as he stepped into the reception area outside his office, opened a large file cabinet and pulled out a file folder. His secretary's desk was empty, Mitch noted.

On a high shelf that ran the circumference of the office were samples of every decoy ever made at

Dennison Ducks, all painted, all different sizes, shapes and types of ducks. The light made the dozens of eyes glitter as if watching him.

Wade handed Mitch the file and returned to his big black leather chair on the other side of the desk.

The folder had little in it. The Dennison Ducks employment application was one page. Under Former Employers, Nina had named a craft shop in Lincoln City called Doodles and a restaurant called The Cove in North Bend along the coast where she'd been a waitress. Not exactly great references for decoy painting, which he'd always heard took a great deal of artistic talent. So why had Nina been hired so quickly at Dennison Ducks?

Nina had left the phone numbers of her past employers blank. Under the space for her former address, she'd just put Lincoln City and the name of a motel or apartment building there, Seashore Views. No address. No phone number.

"There isn't much here," Mitch agreed. "And it doesn't look like she had any experience as a painter."

"She'd done some painting at the craft shop where she worked." Wade sounded defensive. "She just didn't put it down."

Uh-huh. There was *nothing* about painting experience on her application. Nor was there anything under next of kin or a number to call in case of emergency. "What do you know about her personally?"

Wade looked surprised. "Personally? I don't know anything about her."

"You must have talked to her," Mitch said.

"I might have complimented her on a couple of the designs she came to me with, but nothing other than that. I let my group leaders or my secretary handle all personnel problems."

"Were there problems with Nina?" Mitch had to ask.

"None that I know of." Wade seemed to avoid his gaze.

Mitch didn't like the feeling he was getting. "You told me earlier that she didn't have any family or friends or boyfriends."

"That's just what I heard." He straightened several items on his desk, obviously nervous.

"Who is the group leader in the paint department?"

"Sheryl Bends." Sheryl who hadn't said squat the whole time Mitch had asked questions.

"Do you have a photograph of Nina?"

Wade seemed startled by the question. "Why would I have a photo of her?"

"I thought maybe you had some sort of employee card with her photo on it or possibly a photo that was taken at some Dennison Duck function," he suggested.

Wade shook his head. He was perspiring, although the office was quite cool. There were large patches of sweat darkening the underarms of his shirt. "Nina had only worked here a month. She missed the company summer picnic.''

Mitch asked for a copy of the one-page application and a W-9 form she had filled out stating only one deduction, everything that had been in her file. Wade made the copies himself on a small copier just outside his office.

''Where's Ethel?'' Mitch asked, wondering where Wade's secretary was today.

Wade blinked as if he'd been a thousand miles away. ''She's off sick.'' He handed him the copies, his fingers shaking as he did.

The man was awfully upset about an employee he'd hardly known and who'd only worked for him a month.

''Wade,'' he said folding the copies and putting them into his coat pocket, ''I need you to be honest with me. If there's something more going on with Nina—''

Wade waved him off. ''I've got a lot on my mind today, some personal things I need to tend to. I'm just concerned about her, that's all. I don't want anything to have happened to her.''

''Why do you think something has happened to her?'' Mitch asked. Wade didn't know about Nina's ransacked bungalow. Or did he? Wade knew something. That much was clear.

''I just think about Desiree...'' Wade broke off, shook his head and looked away. ''You know, if she was the one missing...''

"How *is* Desiree?" Mitch inquired, pretty sure he already knew the answer. Desiree was twenty-nine and pretty wild.

"Fine," Wade said quickly. "Desiree is fine."

Mitch studied him for a moment. "Okay," he said, and got to his feet, thinking about the baby spoon in his pocket, wondering how to ask about it, deciding now wasn't the time. "If you hear anything…"

Wade glanced at his phone. "I'll call you," he said, seeming anxious to get Mitch out of his office.

As Mitch passed the secretary's desk on his way out, he wondered if Ethel Whiting had ever missed a day of work in her life. Ethel had been with Wade since day one. She probably knew the family better than anyone in town.

Coincidence that she'd called in sick on the day Nina Monroe had gone missing?

The phone rang in Wade's office as Mitch started down the stairs. "It's about time you called," Wade snapped, making Mitch pause on the steps. "Listen to me, Desiree. I've always bailed you out of trouble, but this time you've gone too far. You know damned well what I'm talking about—" The office door closed, cutting off anything further.

Mitch could only imagine what sort of behavior Wade had been referring to. He'd heard stories about Desiree Dennison and her wild antics. Who hadn't? Mitch had picked her up for speeding in that little red sports car on several occasions. Recently she'd reportedly run Sissy's brother T.C. off the road. T.C. made furniture at his small shop outside of town.

Fortunately for Desiree, T.C. hadn't wanted to press charges, but it was obvious that Desiree had purposely forced T.C.'s old pickup off the road because he'd been going too slowly.

Maybe what had Wade upset and concerned this morning was really Desiree, not Nina Monroe. Wade *should* be concerned about Desiree. The woman was headed for trouble, sure as hell.

It was still raining, coming down in sheets, as Mitch stepped outside to find decoy painter Tracy Shank having a cigarette under the overhang of the roof. She glanced around when she saw him as if she thought someone might be watching her and stubbed out the cigarette.

"Did you find out anything?" she asked.

He shook his head. "Nothing more than I already knew."

Tracy lit another cigarette, took a drag and blew the smoke out into the rain. "There's something going on. Something...odd."

"With Nina?"

"With Nina, with Wade, with this place," she said, and glanced over her shoulder. "Nina was no painter. She just showed up one day and Wade hired her. She acted like all she wanted was to learn how to paint decoys. That's why she worked late all the time."

"You don't think that was the case?" he asked.

She let out an oath and shook her head.

"Then why work late?"

"I don't know. The plant is deserted after six. She'd have the whole place to herself. Painters are pretty much allowed to work their own hours, but something else was going on with that girl."

"You think she was meeting someone here? Having an affair? Wouldn't that make more sense at her apartment?" he asked.

"She was living at Florie's," Tracy pointed out. Everyone in town knew how Florie was about minding everyone else's business. It ran in the family. "If she didn't want anyone to know, the plant would be the perfect place."

"No one checks after hours?"

Tracy shook her head. "Doubt Wade's ever needed to. The place is locked up so only employees have access. What employee would be stupid enough to steal a duck? Wouldn't be worth it if you lost your job—plus, we get all the decoys we want at cost. Not that anyone who works here wants to even look at a damned duck after a whole day with them." She took another long drag on her cigarette.

"If Nina was using the plant, who do you think she was meeting here? Wade?"

Tracy made a face. "He's old enough to be her father."

Yeah, that was just what worried Mitch.

"Is there anyone else she might have been romantically involved with?"

Tracy snorted. "Have you seen the guys who work here? The ones who aren't married are all like Bud. Enough said?"

He nodded. "You didn't like Nina."

Tracy looked startled. "I didn't have anything to do with her disappearance, if that's what you're thinking."

He said nothing, waiting.

Tracy finished her cigarette, stubbed out the butt on the concrete and crossed her arms. She looked cold and he realized she'd come outside without her coat, but she didn't appear ready to go back in yet. "I suppose you'll hear about this sooner or later," she said. "Nina and I hung out for a while after she first came to work here."

That surprised him, but he said nothing.

"She befriended *me* and she dropped me as soon as I was no longer useful."

"Useful?"

"She wanted to know a lot of stuff about Dennison Ducks and Wade and the family and everyone who worked here—you know, the good gossip."

He nodded.

"Okay, I screwed up. She and I would have a few beers and I probably talked too much. Hell, I thought she was my friend, all right? How was I to know she would use everything I told her against me?"

Tracy had just given herself a motive if Nina turned up dead, and she must have realized it. "Look, no one liked her. What she did to me was minor compared to the crap she pulled on other people here. She was a user. It made you sick to watch her. Especially the way she played up to Wade.''

''She got special treatment?''

Tracy rolled her eyes. ''I'll say.''

''Why, if Wade wasn't romantically involved with her?''

Tracy shifted her feet and looked out at the rain for a moment. ''It was more like Nina had something on him, you know? He treated her with kid gloves. So did Bud. But you know Bud—he does whatever Wade tells him to.''

Mitch noticed that Tracy was talking about Nina in the past tense. ''You make it sound like you don't think Nina will be back.''

''It would be like her to up and leave town. I always got the feeling that she wasn't planning to stay long, anyway.'' She glanced at her watch. ''I've got to get back in. I need this job.''

''Thanks for your help. Call me if you think of anything else.''

She nodded, but he could tell she was already regretting talking to him. He wouldn't be hearing from *her*.

After she disappeared back into the building, he stood for a moment watching the rain before he sprinted to his patrol car. Once inside, he pulled the papers Wade had given him from his coat pocket, his fingers brushing the baby spoon.

Slowly, he reached into his pocket and palmed the

spoon. It felt cold and oddly heavy, a weight he desperately wanted to shed.

He'd almost asked Wade about it. But the timing had felt wrong. There had to be way to find out if it was indeed Angela Dennison's baby spoon, why Nina Monroe had it hidden under her bureau drawer and finally what, if anything, the spoon might have to do with Nina's disappearance.

Unfortunately all that would have to wait, he thought as a yellow VW bug whipped in behind his patrol car, blocking his exit. He dropped the baby spoon back into his pocket as Charity Jenkins in a hooded clear plastic raincoat with bright red ladybugs on it jumped out and ran through the rain toward his car.

He groaned, struck as always with both desire and worry. What was Charity up to now?

Chapter Five

Charity saw the frown on Mitch's face she associated with broccoli as he opened his door and climbed out into the pouring rain to walk toward her.

"I was just mugged at the post office," she blurted out. So much for her plan to remain calm, not to act hysterical, to keep that wonderful control she associated with normal.

"Mugged?" After all, this *was* Timber Falls.

She pointed at the mud on one side of her jeans as irrefutable evidence she'd been knocked down.

He looked at her jeans, then at her.

She could tell he was struggling with her story. "Someone knocked me down and tried to steal my mail!"

"Is this a joke?" He smiled, making those little crinkles she loved around his incredible sky-blue eyes and those deep Tanner dimples. Rain dripped from his hat and his raincoat. As annoyed as she was, she wished he'd take her in his arms and hold her. For a moment she thought he might.

But then he said, "Let's get out of the rain. Climb in the patrol car and you can tell me what happened."

Brushing a wet lock of hair back under her raincoat hood, she stepped around to the passenger side, opened the door and slid in, steeling herself. Whenever she got within two feet of the man, sparks flew—one way or another.

It was exactly as she knew it would be inside his patrol car. Warm, dry and intimate, with just the hint of his scent, a mixture of soap, rain and maleness. Lots of maleness.

She took a deep breath and let it out slowly, trying to keep her equilibrium. This man was like a washing machine's spin cycle.

He climbed in and started the engine, kicking up the heater. "Okay, you say someone took your mail?"

"Someone knocked me down and then started going through the mail I'd dropped as if he was looking for something." It sounded so improbable to her she couldn't imagine Mitch believing it, which he obviously didn't, judging from his expression.

Which made her all the more determined to make him believe her. "Sarah saw it. She came running out and he took off!"

"With your mail?"

"No," she said. "He dropped it."

"You're sure he was going through it? He wasn't just picking it up and the two of you scared him? There wasn't any yelling or screaming involved, was there?"

He knew her too well. "You know Sarah. She yelled at him. But he *was* going through my mail looking for something." Mitch was starting to irritate her. "That isn't all. I'm pretty sure he took off in a black pickup—the same black pickup that's been following me."

"A black pickup's been *following* you? Since when?"

"I saw it the first time last night just before I went to bed. It followed me to Betty's this morning. And while I was there, it came by twice more, real slow, and I could feel the driver staring at me."

"You *saw* the driver?"

"Well, no. The truck has dark-tinted windows, but I could feel him looking at me."

Kind of the way Mitch was right now. Only Mitch was frowning, too. "Charity," he said with obvious patience, "there are a lot of strangers in town because of this Bigfoot thing, people just driving around, looking around."

There was no convincing him. Worse, she wondered now if he could be right. But then, that would make her wrong. "The truck was definitely following me."

"Charity, how can you be sure if you didn't even see his face? He could have been looking for someone in the café. Someone other than you."

"Right. And he was looking for that same person in front of my house last night? Why is it so hard for you to believe me?" she demanded, annoyed with him, annoyed even more that her story did sound hard to believe, now that she'd said it out loud. Not that she would admit it to him. "The driver of the pickup was *following* me and then he attacked me outside the post office."

Mitch sighed. "You said you *thought* the man who knocked you down got into a black pickup?"

"I didn't see him get in it, no. But I saw a black pickup down the street a few moments later."

He raised a brow and she wondered if someone had told him about her earlier mistaken encounter with the *wrong* black pickup. Liam wouldn't tell on her. But that Emily would.

"Fine. Don't believe me. But I think the driver is the same person who left the present on my doorstep."

"I thought you were convinced I left it."

"Well, you obviously didn't, so now I think it was the guy in the black truck."

"You noticed this pickup last night, you say? But you didn't bother to mention any of this when we talked earlier this morning. Maybe the present was left on your doorstep by mistake."

Oh, that was so like him. "You just can't believe that I might have a...a...secret admirer, can you?"

"That's not it," he said.

She opened the passenger-side door. "I thought you might want to find this black pickup before he does more than mug me and try to steal my mail, but since you don't believe me—"

"Hold on," Mitch said, his voice low and soft and

sexy as ever. "Give me a description of the person who knocked you down at the post office."

"*Mugged* me. He was big or at least his raincoat was big. He had his back to me and his hood up, so I never saw his face or his body really."

"It was a man? Not some kid?"

"Yes, it was a man. A big man. Or a really big woman."

Mitch groaned. "Were there any checks or money orders in your mail?"

"I don't know. I just glanced at it. I didn't see anything interesting. I'm pretty sure it was all bills."

He nodded, obviously wondering why anyone would steal her bills. Good question. "So he looked through your mail."

"He dropped it when Sarah came out." She knew what Mitch was thinking. That the person hadn't meant to knock her down, that it was just an accident.

But that didn't explain the black pickup following her. "Just forget it." She shoved open the door and propelled herself out into the pouring rain. "I'll find the truck myself." She slammed the door and stomped toward her car.

"Charity!" he called after her.

She heard his door open, but she didn't turn. She climbed into her VW, her hands shaking with anger as she fumbled for the key. That man was impossible. Worse, she feared she'd done it again. Acted irrationally and confirmed Mitch's suspicions that she was a flake just like the rest of her family.

Was it possible that the truck wasn't following

her? That the man at the post office had accidentally knocked her down and was only picking up her mail when she and Sarah yelled at him? Was it possible she, Charity Jenkins, had overreacted?

"Charity." Mitch was at her side window looking down at her, water pouring off his hat, his expression pained. "Roll down your window. Please," he said through the drumming rain.

She finally found the key and turned it. The VW engine started. She wanted to throw the car into reverse and go racing out of there, but she rolled down her window.

"I'm sorry," he said, then looked past her to the passenger-side seat. "Is that the present?"

"Yes."

"Let me see it."

She carefully handed the box with the stone heart in it to him and he stuck it inside his coat.

"Did you handle the stone?" he asked, then looked at her and groaned as if he knew she had. "Well, there might be other prints."

Rain was coming in the window but she hardly noticed. "Yeah, maybe." She was touched that he was at least acting as if he was taking her seriously. That was something, right? Even if he was just humoring her?

"Can you think of any reason someone would be following you? Have an interest in your mail? Or leave you this?"

"No."

"What does this black pickup look like?"

"Older model, black with dark-tinted windows. I didn't see the plate. There was too much mud on it."

He looked at her and she could feel that old chemistry bubbling between them and knew he could, too. But chemistry wasn't the problem. It was the M-word: marriage. She had to hold out for it. No matter how strong the pull. She couldn't let Mitch talk her into anything short of holy matrimony. But right now, just the thought of being snuggled in his arms...

"If you see this pickup again, try to get a license-plate number for me. Or a description of the driver. But don't take any chances. Call me at once."

She nodded, then remembered Wade Dennison had been seen coming out of Mitch's office earlier. Wade, according to her source, had looked upset, and Mitch was up here at the plant. Now why was that?

"Something's going on with Wade Dennison, isn't it?" she asked, and saw his expression change ever so slightly. Oh, she did love it when she was right. Something *was* up! Her journalistic nose for news smelled a story. "What's going on?"

"How did you know I was out here?" he asked, frowning through the rain.

"I can't reveal my sources. Pretend I followed you."

"Speaking of being followed by a dangerous person..." He shook his head as if he'd finally figured out that lecturing her was a waste of breath, but the corners of his mouth turned up a little. His warm fingers squeezed her shoulder. "Call me if you see the truck," he said, and trotted back to his patrol car.

Charity drove back into town, warmed all over even though still muddy and wet from being attacked at the post office—and sitting with her window down talking to Mitch. His touch always sent sparks shooting through her body and a warmth better than her VW heater.

She had interviewed Frank, the Granny's bread deliveryman late last night, but she hadn't written the story yet. She reminded herself that she had a paper to put out, but first she needed to change into some dry clothes. Then she could worry about what Mitch was doing at Dennison Ducks.

Meanwhile, she kept an eye out for the black pickup. There was always the chance she wasn't overreacting.

MITCH WATCHED Charity drive away, remembering what she'd said about the person who'd knocked her down outside the post office. It had to have been an accident. This was Timber Falls. People didn't get mugged.

But as he glanced over at the red heart-shaped stone in the package on the seat next to him, he couldn't shake the bad feeling he had. Charity in some sort of trouble? What were the chances?

He started the patrol car and followed her at an inconspicuous distance back into town. She went straight home. Since he lived just next door, he pulled into his own driveway and waited until she was safely inside her house. But even then he couldn't bring himself to leave and kept watching the street behind him for a black pickup.

Fifteen minutes later, she emerged in clean jeans, climbed into her VW and drove to her office uptown. If she noticed him, which she must have, she didn't let on.

He figured she'd be safe at her office since she was only down the block. He needed to find out more about Nina Monroe.

Back at his own office, he double-checked Nina Monroe's social security number from her Dennison Ducks employment application. Same as the invalid one Wade had given him earlier.

He called her references. The manager of Doodles, the craft shop where she said she'd worked, had never heard of her. Nor did the woman recognize the description Mitch gave him. The same with The Cove in North Bend and Seashore Views apartment complex in Lincoln City. He hung up, wishing he had a photograph. But he doubted it would have done any good. Obviously all the information on Nina's application was bogus. So who *was* she?

He hated to think.

After he'd exhausted all law-enforcement avenues, he put on his coat again and headed for the door, knowing the one person who might be able to help him.

WADE DENNISON'S secretary lived in a big old Victorian at the end of Main. Ethel Whiting's roots could be traced back to before Timber Falls was even a town, when it was nothing more than a logging camp. Her father had been one of the town's founders. He'd married well, but brought only one child into the world, a daughter, Ethel. His only heir.

Ethel still lived in the house where she was born. In fact, she'd never left. Right after high school, she'd gone to work and taken care of her aging parents, until both passed on.

Now in her early seventies, Ethel didn't need to work—at least not for the money. She was probably the richest woman in town. It was rumored she'd helped Wade Dennison start the decoy plant years ago. Others swore it had been Wade's new bride, Daisy, who'd footed the bill. Either way, Ethel had been a permanent fixture at Dennison Ducks ever since.

The decoy business had grown and so had the town as the demand for decoys grew and Dennison Ducks became famous.

Mitch hurried through the rain to the front door of the well-kept Victorian, rang the bell and waited. If Ethel really was sick…

She opened the door immediately. Almost as if she'd been expecting him. ''Mitchell,'' she said. She was the only person besides his mother who'd ever called him that. ''Do come in.''

He stepped into the cool darkness of the house. It smelled of furniture polish and fresh-perked coffee. As Ethel motioned him into the parlor, he caught the hint of lilac perfume.

She wore a blue cotton dress, sensible shoes and

a white cardigan with tiny blue-and-white flowers on it. Her gray hair was neatly pulled back in a bun from her heart-shaped face. It was obvious she'd once been a real beauty.

"Would you care for a cup of coffee?" she asked after offering him one of the antique chairs in the dark and austere parlor. He doubted the decor had changed since her parents' day.

"I'd love a cup, if it's not too much trouble."

"I just made a pot. Please make yourself comfortable."

It surprised him that she lived alone. She'd never married or hired a companion or any help. She was much too independent and self-sufficient for that. He thought it too bad more women weren't like her—then he thought of Charity and that overconfidence and irritating independence of hers. Maybe it was better more women didn't have it.

"You don't take cream or sugar, as I recall," Ethel said, putting down a silver tray. She poured the coffee, handing him a fine China cup and saucer.

"You have a good memory." He took a sip, the China feeling fragile in his big hands. "I'd forgotten how good perked coffee tastes."

"Did you stop by to compliment my coffee?"

"No, I'm here for the same reason you made a fresh pot. You knew I'd be asking you about Nina Monroe."

She nodded. "I understand she's missing?"

He nodded. "Tell me about her."

Ethel raised a brow. "She's only been employed at Dennison Ducks for a little over a month."

"And caused a lot of trouble during that time."

"You are well-informed."

"Is there any truth to it?" he asked.

"Truth to what?"

Age didn't seem to matter when it came to getting straight answers from women, he thought. "That Nina could easily be Wade Dennison's downfall?"

"You're asking if Nina had some kind of hold on him...." Her blue eyes darkened and she nodded. "I saw it and tried to warn Wade about her." She sighed and picked up her cup and saucer to take a dainty sip of her coffee.

He noticed that her hands were shaking. "Wade didn't take kindly to your concern?"

"He reminded me yesterday that I was only his secretary."

Mitch was surprised. If there was any truth to the rumor that she'd helped Wade start the business, she must have been furious. And hurt. "I'm surprised he'd say that to you."

"I was, too." She paused. "I'm very concerned for him."

"Not for Nina?"

"Nina, it seems, can take care of herself."

"You didn't like her."

Ethel's only response was a tight smile.

"I've never known you to miss a day of work."

"I've never known you not to say what's on your mind, Mitchell."

"You aren't sick."

"No, I resigned yesterday."

He was shocked. "After you spoke to Wade about Nina?" And before Nina's disappearance, he thought.

She nodded. "I should have retired a long time ago. Wade just helped me realize that the time was right."

"Was Wade's attitude toward Nina the only reason?"

She put down her cup and saucer and folded her hands in her lap. "It was time."

"Ethel, I need to ask you something and I'm not sure how. You've been close to the Dennisons for years."

"I've known Wade all my life."

"You probably remember when Desiree was born." She nodded and he continued, "Wade had special silverware designed for her. Then another set made when Angela was born two years later. Ones with duck's heads on them?"

"A spoon and a fork engraved with each girl's name. Hart's Jewelry in Eugene made them just for Wade."

"Then Daisy probably still has them."

Ethel shook her head. "Wade ordered everything of Angela's to be discarded. He couldn't bear to see anything that reminded him of his daughter."

"When was this?" Mitch asked.

"A few weeks after the baby disappeared. By that time, he was convinced Angela wouldn't be returned, and every time Daisy saw something of the baby's, she became upset.''

Wade's compassion for his wife surprised Mitch. Especially if the rumors were true and baby Angela hadn't even been Wade's. Whatever the case, Daisy had been a recluse, hiding in that big old house for the past twenty-seven years, ever since her daughter's disappearance.

''Wade didn't keep even Angela's baby silver?''

She shook her head. ''Not as far as I know. He took everything of the baby's to the dump and buried it himself. I remember the day all too well. I'd never seen Wade so...devastated.'' Her eyes shone with tears and her cheeks were heightened with color.

Mitch stared at Ethel, wondering why he'd never seen it before. She was in love with Wade! Ethel was a good five years older than Wade. Not that the age difference mattered when it came to love. Mitch wondered if Wade knew. According to Sissy, men could be dense as tree stumps when it came to this sort of thing.

''You don't think Daisy squirreled away something of Angela's?'' he asked. ''Or maybe Wade did at the last moment?''

Ethel shook her head. ''Why are you asking about this now?''

''I found what I believe is Angela's baby spoon. It was in Nina's bungalow, taped under a dresser drawer.''

She took in a sharp breath, her eyes suddenly hard

and cold. "I haven't heard Angela's name even whispered in years, and now this."

"Is it possible Nina is Angela?" If he'd expected Ethel to be surprised by the question, he would have been wrong.

She didn't even blink. "It is possible Wade *believed* it. Or wished it were true."

"You don't believe she's Angela?"

Ethel smiled. "It really doesn't matter what I believe, does it, Mitchell?"

"It does to me."

She straightened and took a breath, her gaze steely. "If Nina Monroe is the baby who was stolen from her crib at the Dennison house twenty-seven years ago, then it's best if we never know it."

"I don't understand."

"Nina Monroe is...flawed. Maybe she was born that way. Maybe life made her that way. It doesn't matter really. Either way, if she is Angela Dennison, then it's a dark day for the Dennison family."

"Flawed how?"

"I believe she is capable of doing *anything* to get what she wants. No matter who she hurts. She is a dangerous woman who won't stop until she destroys herself and anyone who gets in her path."

He felt a chill curl around his neck. "What does she want?"

"Money, position. Everything she's been denied."

He stared at her. "She wants to be...Angela Dennison?"

Ethel raised a brow. "If it gets her what she feels she deserves."

He didn't like what he was hearing. If Ethel was right and Nina wanted to be Angela Dennison— might actually be Angela—who in town would try to stop her?

Ethel Whiting for one, he thought. She would do whatever it took to protect Wade, he realized with a start.

He'd learned a long time ago to leave the hard questions until last. That way if he got thrown out, he'd at least have some answers.

"I took a look at the old case file on Angela Dennison's disappearance," he said carefully. "Wade was a suspect. It seems there was a rumor circulating that Angela wasn't his and he knew it."

Ethel got to her feet and drew herself up to her full height. "Wade Dennison can be a fool, he's proved that. But he wouldn't have hurt that baby. Even if it wasn't his."

"Was it his?"

"Were either of them his? I guess that's something you'd have to ask his wife." She met his gaze, making one thing perfectly clear: there was no love lost between Ethel and Daisy.

"Thanks for the coffee. It was wonderful. I'd appreciate it if you didn't…"

"I wouldn't dream of carrying this conversation outside these walls," Ethel said primly.

"Sorry, it's habit. But if you should think of anyone who might know something about Nina…"

"I wouldn't rule out Nina staging her own disappearance," Ethel said. "Or using Charity to get what she wants."

"Charity?"

"Yes. She was asking questions about Nina at the plant yesterday."

He was stunned. Charity had been asking questions about Nina Monroe the day she disappeared? "What kind of questions?"

Ethel shook her head. "She didn't talk to me. I think she knows I would never talk about Dennison Duck business with a reporter. You'll have to ask her."

He turned to leave, anxious to find Charity and do just that.

"Mitchell."

He felt Ethel's fingers dig into his arm.

"Whatever you do, don't underestimate Nina—or what she's capable of." Ethel's words vibrated with emotion. "Be careful. Very careful."

He nodded, surprised by the concern he heard in her voice.

"You know where you can find me if you should...need to," she said, and released his arm, appearing almost embarrassed by her little outburst as she turned away.

Chapter Six

Charity looked up from her computer, surprised to see Mitch come through the newspaper-office door. He appeared upset.

"You found the black pickup?" she cried, getting to her feet. Or did his visit have something to do with that stupid present?

"Why were you asking questions about Nina Monroe?" he demanded.

She stared at him. "What?"

"It's true, isn't it?"

Where had he heard that? And more important, why was he so upset? "Unless I'm mistaken, you and I don't talk about much of anything anymore. And you certainly haven't shown any interest in my newspaper articles."

"You were doing an article on Nina?"

He wasn't going to tell her that there really was a story there, was he? "Why do you care?"

He pulled off his hat, raked a hand through his hair and groaned. "I just found out that you were asking questions about her the day she disappeared."

Charity blinked. *"Disappeared?"* Holy moly, maybe there really was a story.

"Nina didn't show up for work this morning, and Wade is worried that something's happened to her."

Charity lowered herself into a chair, her mind reeling. "I'd heard rumors about the new painter at the plant but—"

"What kind of rumors?"

She looked up at him. "Rumors that something was going on between her and Wade."

"And?"

"And nothing. I asked a few questions, didn't get any answers." Had she missed something? Obviously. "I was going to do a feature on her. She'd promised to write down a few things for me and get back to me."

"Charity, if you know anything about Nina Monroe's disappearance, now is the time to tell me."

She wished she did. "I haven't a clue, really."

He sighed, eyeing her suspiciously. "It just seems odd that you would be asking questions about her on the day she was last seen."

Yes, it did. She glanced at her watch.

"What?" he demanded.

"I was just thinking." Her stomach rumbled.

"About food?" He sounded incredulous.

She smiled. "You know me *so* well."

"Charity, I don't have time for even a late lunch."

"I had Betty put back two pieces of lemon-meringue pie." She gave him her most seductive smile, hoping that, combined with lemon-meringue pie, she'd be irresistible.

"You were that sure we'd be having lunch together?"

"I guess some things are destined, Mitch, especially if you want to continue this discussion," she said, and went to get her raincoat before he could argue the point.

Mitch told himself that he had to eat. Also, he knew he'd get more answers out of her on a full stomach—hers, not his. And there was something about Nina Monroe she wasn't telling him.

BECAUSE IT WAS the middle of the afternoon, Betty's Café was relatively empty. Everyone was probably out looking for Bigfoot.

He and Charity took a booth at the back and ordered their usual: cheeseburgers, loaded, and French fries, the kind that were hot and greasy and made from potatoes that still had their skins on when they hit the boiling grease.

It reminded him of when they were in high school. Those were good memories. In fact, when he thought about it, he could call up lots of good memories with Charity. But they were before she'd become the town reporter and he'd become the sheriff, before he'd realized that marrying her would be nothing less than disastrous given their families and their genes.

"All right, let's hear it," he said, after he'd watched Charity put away most of her burger and fries.

With her fingers, she dragged a long greasy French fry through a pool of ketchup and took a bite, closing her eyes as if eating for her was an erotic experience. He had a feeling it probably was. Just watching her definitely did something to him.

She smiled as her eyes opened, focusing on him in a way that made him more than a little uneasy.

"Nina," he reminded her quietly. Betty was busy helping the cook finish up the dinner special and so was out of earshot. But this *was* Timber Falls. And Betty had amazing hearing.

Charity swallowed the bite, putting down the French fry to wipe her hands on her napkin.

He reached across the table to whisk away the drop of ketchup at the corner of her mouth. She did have the most wonderful mouth, bow-shaped lips full and luscious.

He shook himself mentally, knowing where thinking like that would get him. A cold shower. How many times had Charity made it abundantly clear: marriage or nothing. Nothing but frustration.

She gave him a smile now and licked the spot where he'd touched her lips. The woman was incorrigible.

"*Charity.*"

"I already told you. I heard rumors about Nina and Wade, about her not being too popular out at the plant, and I decided to do a story on her."

"And?"

Charity picked up another fry and eyed him, smiling. "Your turn. Tell me what you've found out."

"It doesn't work that way and you know it."

"It should." She took a bite.

He groaned. "Her bungalow at your aunt's was ransacked." He figured Florie would tell Charity, anyway. "Your turn. Was Wade having an affair with Nina?"

"I don't think so, and frankly, most of what I heard about Nina sounded like sour grapes among a few employees trying to make trouble for her and Wade, especially Sheryl. She'd be my first suspect if Nina really is missing."

He wished now he hadn't said anything. All he'd done was alert Charity to a possible story. But then again, Nina had done that by disappearing. He was reminded of what Ethel had said. Was this just a way for Nina to call attention to herself? Had she ransacked her own bungalow, leaving the baby spoon for him to find, knowing Wade would involve the sheriff when she didn't show up for work? And maybe she'd helped along the rumors about her and Wade just to get Charity involved. Ethel had said Nina might be using Charity. Nina had agreed to an interview. If Nina was Angela Dennison, maybe Nina hoped Charity would break the story.

He frowned. "You said Nina was going to write something down for you? Like what?"

Charity shrugged. "She said she'd had an interesting life. *Everybody* thinks their life would make a good book. What would make Wade think Nina met with foul play?"

He shrugged.

She wasn't buying it. "Maybe there *was* something going on between them."

"I don't think so." He tried to think of something to change the subject.

Charity looked disappointed but not deterred. "It would explain why Wade hired her without any experience and so quickly, why he seemed to think she could do no wrong, even why he's so worried about her now, huh?"

Yeah, that was one explanation all right.

"But then there's the gun she bought for protection," Charity said.

"Gun?" It wasn't registered to Nina Monroe or it would have come up on the computer. And why had she thought she needed protection?

"She showed it to Hank Bridges one night at the Duck-In."

"She showed it to the *bartender?*" He definitely didn't like the sound of this.

"I guess she'd had quite a lot to drink—she was the last to leave the bar. Hank was worried about her getting home safely. She told him she could take care of herself, then opened her purse and showed him the gun."

"What kind of gun?"

"You know Hank." She rolled her eyes. Hank Bridges still lived with his parents. His mother, Sarah, was Timber Falls's postmistress, and Buzz, his father, was a carver out at Dennison Ducks. His younger brother, Blaine, was still in high school and worked part-time for Charity. Neither young man was what you'd call manly. Hank, especially, was scared to death of guns and spiders and, well, most everything outdoors.

"Hank didn't know what kind of gun it was."

Charity nodded. "Just said it was small but lethal-looking."

"When was this?"

"Saturday night."

"What if Nina did write something down and mailed it to me?" she cried.

He stared at her. "Like what?"

"Her life history. Or maybe why she was carrying a gun for protection?" Charity suggested.

"Sounds like a long shot."

"But it's a theory, anyway."

Charity and her theories.

He swore under his breath. Just a few nights before Nina disappeared she'd been at the Duck-In drinking too much and waving around a firearm? She'd also had an argument with some man at her bungalow earlier Tuesday evening, according to Florie. "She happen to mention to Hank why she thought she needed protection?"

Charity wagged her head. "Hank didn't *want* to know."

"That's everything you know about Nina?"

She nodded.

He studied her. Why did he get the feeling she still wasn't telling him everything? Because she was Charity.

"You can't really keep me from doing this story, you know," she said.

He knew. It would soon be public knowledge that one of Dennison Ducks painters had gone missing. He couldn't keep Charity from printing that.

What worried him now was that Charity would go after the story like the bloodhound she was. He groaned at the thought, remembering what Ethel had said.

"This could be dangerous," he warned.

Charity arched a brow. "I'm a journalist. We don't back off from a story because it might be dangerous. It would be like you refusing to do your job for the same reason."

Right. "Okay, how are your sisters?" he asked, knowing he wasn't going to change her mind. Not Charity. And the harder he pushed, the more determined she would become.

"Why are you asking about my sisters?" she questioned suspiciously. "Is one of them missing, too?"

"No, I just…" He wished now he'd simply eaten his pie and said nothing. "I was just curious. I saw Hope a while back, that's all."

Charity was still eyeing him as if he'd only brought up her family as an example of why the two of them were so wrong for each other. Her crazy family. Not to mention his own. And all he'd wanted to do was change the subject. "Hope told me she split up with her boyfriend."

Charity made a face. "Good riddance. She deserved better."

"You've seen her, then?" he asked, surprised. He got the impression that Charity tried to distance herself from her family—as if that would change her DNA.

"Hope drove up one night last week, brought a bottle of wine and a pizza from the Duck-In. We both got a little tipsy and giggly." She smiled in memory.

He wished he'd seen that. He could just imagine Charity's full lips stained red with wine. Damn, but he missed kissing her.

Charity pulled her piece of lemon-meringue pie close enough so she could get a fork into it. She gazed down at the bite with nothing short of worship. "Her boyfriend turned out to be a real bastard." She put the bite in her mouth, closed her lips on the tines and shut her eyes as she slowly withdrew the fork from between her lips.

He groaned inwardly as he watched her and tried damned hard not to remember a time he'd been responsible for putting that look on her face. "How was he a bastard?"

She opened her eyes, grimaced as if disappointed. "Tart?" he asked.

Her eyes widened. "You say the sweetest things."

"I meant the pie."

She smiled and took another bite, obviously knowing only too well what he meant. She didn't close her eyes this time. "I think her boyfriend took advantage of her."

Mitch felt himself squirm. "In what way?"

She looked over at him, her gaze locking with his.

Her eyes were warm honey, flecked with equal amounts sunbeams and mischief. "He wanted her—just not badly enough to marry her."

"The *bastard*," Mitch said.

"Funny." She took another bite of pie.

Speaking of boyfriends… "Do you know if Nina was seeing anyone?"

Charity shook her head.

Damn. He could see the wheels turning. He'd given her something else to go after, and Charity was amazing at finding out information. "If you should learn anything more about Nina or her disappearance…"

She smiled at him. "I have your number."

Yeah. He glanced at his watch, then at her. Time to go. But he hesitated. That stupid red heart-shaped stone bothered him, as did Charity's story about the black pickup and the man who'd knocked her down at the post office.

Mitch feared that the black pickup and the man at the post office were somehow tied in with Nina's disappearance. If Nina really had disappeared. He was still holding out hope that she'd show up before dark.

"Also, if you see that black pickup or get any more gifts…" He couldn't help but worry about Charity, especially given that she'd been asking questions about Nina the day the painter had disappeared. Except what could he do? Lock Charity up? Not let her out of his sight? "You're going back to your office?"

She nodded.

"Is Blaine coming in to help put the paper together tonight?"

Charity smiled at his concern, eating it up like pie. "I won't be alone, if that's what you're worried about."

He started to deny that he worried about her, but saved his breath as he picked up his hat from the seat beside him, settled it on his head and looked at her. "Lunch was a good idea."

"Lunch is always a good idea," she said, and smiled up at him as he slid from the booth. She had a killer smile. It had nearly done him in more times than he wanted to remember.

He stood for a moment just looking at her, tempted. Tempted to ask her to the community-center dance next weekend. Tempted to see what she was doing for dinner tonight. Just plain tempted.

But then the strangest thing happened. He heard wedding bells. It was only the old bell ringing down at the church signaling school was out, but the effect was like a cold shower.

"See ya," he said, and tried not to run as he left.

Charity let out a long sigh and fought to slow her pounding pulse. The man had no idea what he did to her. Thank heaven. If she showed even the slightest weakness, she'd be a goner.

"How was it?" Betty asked, sliding into the seat Mitch had just vacated. She wasn't asking about the food.

Charity couldn't help grinning at the older woman. "Nice. Sweet. I think I'm getting to him."

Betty laughed and shook her head. "I would have given up on that man years ago."

"Can't."

"Hell, girl, there's dozens of men who could curl your toes if you'd just let them." Betty gave her a sympathetic look. "Some men just aren't the marrying kind, hon. Mitch thinks he's...damaged goods because of his folks. You know that. Marriage scares him. Maybe especially with you."

Charity nodded. She knew only too well how Mitch felt. "Then I guess I'll be an old maid."

Betty howled at that, sliding out of the booth as a group of out-of-towners came in the door. They shook off raindrops as they inquired about the blue plate special and where exactly Frank, the bread deliveryman, had seen Bigfoot.

Charity sat for a moment, seriously considering the idea of being an old maid. It didn't have much appeal. But it would be *all* Mitch's fault. That was some consolation.

As she started to leave, she saw the black pickup. It cruised by slowly, then took off as if the driver had seen her watching him.

She made a dash for her car, parked down the block in front of the newspaper. Her hands were shaking as she leaped behind the wheel. The engine turned over immediately and she whipped out into the street.

She could see the black truck turn right at the end

of Main onto Mill Creek Road. She took off in pursuit, fumbling to dial the Sheriff's Department number on her cell phone as she did.

"Sheriff's Department," Sissy said, sounding half-asleep.

"Where's Mitch?" Charity demanded, heart pounding.

Sissy sighed her Oh-it's-you-again sigh. "Out on patrol." Mitch could have been in the john or even dead and Sissy still would have said that.

Charity swung a right just past the Spit Curl. The pickup was already past town, headed out the narrow road that led to Dennison Ducks and beyond.

"Get word to Mitch that I found the pickup. He'll know what I'm talking about. I'm chasing it. We're headed east toward the plant. Tell him to hurry!"

That's when she saw the second present. It was stuck to the passenger seat of her car by one long sharp thorn. A bright red rose.

"WHAT THE HELL is that woman thinking?" Mitch demanded when he got the call over the radio a few minutes later.

"We're talking Charity here," Sissy retorted.

Mitch swore as he found a place to turn around. He'd stopped by the post office and talked to Sarah Bridges. She hadn't gotten a look at the person who'd knocked Charity down in the parking lot. In fact, like Charity, she couldn't even be sure it was a man. Just someone in a big dark hooded raincoat.

After that, he'd driven around town, thinking he

might come across Nina's red compact. Wade didn't have a plate number. Just a description of the vehicle. And without Nina's real name…

But Mitch hadn't seen the car. Or a black pickup. Or anyone walking down the highway in a dark rain-coat and looking suspicious.

He had, however, been counting the reasons he should stay clear of Charity Jenkins. There were many. At the top of the list was the fact that the woman lacked good sense and, worse, stole his rea-son, as well. When he was around her, it was as if she'd drugged him, his desire for her a lethal dose that would kill him eventually if he wasn't careful.

He reached the turnoff and headed toward Denni-son Ducks as he tried to calculate how far behind Charity he was. He knew that if she chased the pickup past the plant, she could be in real trouble. The area was isolated, the logging road narrow and seldom used. A person could get lost just a few feet off the road up there, the vegetation was so thick.

Didn't she realize how dangerous this was? Chas-ing a vehicle and driver she thought was following her? What kind of sense did that make?

What worried him the most was that Charity would be acting on impulse—after all it *was* Charity—and not even considering that the pickup might be leading her into a trap. If the driver of the black pickup had some reason to get Charity on an isolated road alone, she'd just played right into his hands.

Just before he reached Dennison Ducks, he tried

her cell-phone number. Either out of the calling area. Or turned off. Great.

Sissy had told him that she'd heard Charity had accosted Liam Sawyer earlier. Liam's new wife had called to complain. Maybe Charity was now chasing Liam.

But that didn't explain the red heart-shaped stone that someone had left for her or the note: THINKING OF YOU. Both worried him.

Charity was in trouble. He could feel it.

As he passed the Dennison Ducks parking lot, he looked to see if either rig was there. No black truck. No yellow VW bug. He swore and kept going, driving as fast as he could, considering the rain was making the narrow muddy road even more treacherous.

He tried not to think about what would happen if Charity caught up with the truck and driver. She wouldn't have thought that far ahead, knowing her. Damn, why did she always have to be so impulsive and take matters into her own hands?

He felt a stab of guilt. It wasn't just her screwball genes. He hadn't really bought her story and she knew it. He'd had a rational explanation for the present, the attack at the post office, the mysterious black truck she said was following her.

Now, knowing Charity, she was dead set on proving to him that she was right—even if it killed her.

He hoped to hell she was wrong this time, though. If the black pickup really had been following her...

He came around a corner in the road and hit his brakes. The VW bug was sitting sideways in the middle of the road, the driver's-side door hanging open, the interior light on, but even from here, he could see that the car was empty.

Dear Lord, where was Charity?

Chapter Seven

Charity bailed off the mountainside on foot, clutching her camera to her breast, pretty sure she'd lost her mind.

Not far up the road, she'd realized—belatedly—that there was a good chance the driver of the pickup was leading her into a trap. He'd left the red rose in her car. Had he also made sure she saw him? Because he wanted her to chase him?

It definitely looked that way. He'd taken a road that was seldom used, and while it eventually wound back around and came out on the highway into Timber Falls, there was a lot of remote country between here and there.

He was drawing her deeper into that country. The truth was, he could have lost her easily since he was driving a vehicle that could go faster than hers.

But at the same time, she desperately wanted to find out who he was—and prove to Mitch the man in the black pickup existed.

That was when the desperate idea had struck her. As the truck disappeared around a curve in the road ahead, she slammed on her brakes, grabbed her camera from the case, got out of her car and dropped over the side of the road down through the thick tangle of underbrush and trees.

The plan was simple. She would cut off the pickup on foot. The truck would soon reach a hairpin curve and loop back directly below the spot where she'd left the VW.

All she had to do was drop straight down the mountainside on foot, push through the jungle of growth, keep from killing herself and reach the road below before the pickup did. Then she could hide in the bushes and get a shot of the pickup—and driver—as both went by.

She'd come this far and she was going to get a photograph of the truck to show Mitch, or die trying.

The idea had seemed inspired at the time.

Now, committed in more ways than one, more out of control than in, trying to protect the camera and save her own life, she crashed down the steep mountainside through the soaking wet foliage, ready to admit it had been a less-than-brilliant plan.

"Eek!" she squealed when, too late, she saw the huge spider web and pretty much fell through it. Frantically she brushed at the silken threads on her face and hair, her raincoat hood falling back, as she continued her downward plunge through the wet ferns and pine boughs, with no chance of stopping. All she could hope was to stay on her feet in the rotting maple leaves.

Sometimes she scared herself with her harebrained

ideas. At these moments, she could kind of see why the thought of marriage to her scared Mitch.

In the distance, she thought she heard the pickup's engine. Soon it would be on the road directly below her. She couldn't see the road yet. Then again, she couldn't see five feet in front of her because of the forest, but she knew she had to be getting close.

She just hoped she didn't come crashing out of the trees and dense brush only to be run down by the truck. Regrettably it appeared she might reach the road at the same time as the black pickup.

And at some point she'd thought this plan was inspired? She was about to find out the driver's intentions—and in the worst possible place. That was if she didn't break her neck before she reached the road. And he didn't run over her.

That was when she heard it. Something crashing through the trees and brush just below her on the mountain. Something *big*. She caught a glimpse of brown fur.

Her breath caught in her throat as she grabbed at tree branches, trying to stop her descent, thoughts of the black pickup replaced by the terrifying thought of colliding with a bear.

Unfortunately she was moving too fast down the precipitous slope to decelerate at all.

Suddenly she broke through the thick cover, bursting out of the trees in a flurry of fern fronds, pine needles and dried leaves, arms and legs flailing. She crashed down in the middle of the road, somehow managing to stay on her feet as she stumbled to a stop. Then she heard the sound of the pickup truck's engine coming closer.

In that instant, something large and dark streaked across the road just inches in front of the pickup's chrome grill. She didn't even realize that she'd jerked the camera up, could barely hear the sound of its motor drive over the thunder of her heart and the screech of the pickup's brakes. Between her and the pickup's grill was something big, dark and furry.

The pickup skidded on the wet muddy road, the grill coming closer and closer and closer to where Charity stood. *Snap, snap, snap.*

At the very last moment, she dove into the dense growth below the road, hugging the camera protectively to her chest as she tumbled a half-dozen yards down the mountainside, disappearing in the dense greenery. When she finally stopped, she lay very still.

Above her, she heard the pickup come to a stop a few yards past where she'd bailed out. Heard the truck door open with a groan. Heard the slap of footsteps through the mud puddles. The sound of heavy breathing. A limb snapped directly above her at the edge of the road, and she knew the driver was standing up there looking down at the spot where she lay hidden in the ferns. At least she hoped she was hidden.

MITCH LEAPED from his patrol car, weapon drawn, as he rushed to Charity's VW. The car was indeed empty, and the keys were still in the ignition.

Whatever had happened here, Charity hadn't had

time to even grab her purse. It was on the seat next to— His heart stuck in his throat as he saw the red rose speared to the passenger seat.

"Oh, God," he breathed. "Charity?" His voice cracked. *"Charity!"*

A blue jay answered from the dripping trees overhead. Rain fell through the lush green canopy and pattered on the forest floor. Over it, he heard what sounded like a car door slam, then the roar of an engine below him on the mountain. Damn. "Charity!"

He hurriedly climbed into the VW, started the engine and pulled the car out of the way, then he rushed back to his patrol car and took off down the road after the sound of the retreating engine.

Not far past the hairpin curve, he spotted her. A small soaked figure in a dirt-covered ladybug-printed raincoat walking up the road toward him. She was hunched forward, clutching her chest.

He threw on his brakes and was out of the patrol car, running toward her before he even realized it.

She looked like a drowned rat, her long auburn hair plastered to her face, her hood thrown back.

As he approached her, he saw that her hair was full of wet leaves and twigs, her ladybug plastic raincoat in tatters and her face scratched and bleeding.

His heart jerked in his chest at the sight of her, and all he wanted to do was take her in his arms.

"Are you all right?" He barely got the words out before he saw what she had clutched to her chest. Her camera. He'd been wrong back at her car. She'd managed to grab at least one thing before she left the car.

She nodded at him, lifting the camera, her lips turning up in a grin. "I got a photo of the black pickup."

He stopped short of her, just short of gathering her in his arms and crushing her to him. *"You what?"*

"I got a photo of the truck that was following me. I had to cut down the mountain through the brush to get the shot, but I did it," she said triumphantly.

He fought the urge to turn her over his knee and spank her. "Have you completely lost your mind?" he demanded.

She brushed a lock of wet hair from her eyes. "What did you expect me to do?"

"With you, Charity, I never know what to expect." He shook his head. She could have been killed. Coming down that mountainside on foot was dangerous enough, but actually getting a photo of the pickup she thought had been following her?

"When you yelled for me, you scared him off," she said. "And just in time." She shivered and looked away. "Thanks."

He took several deep breaths and counted to ten, still so angry he wanted to throttle her. She was all right. Safe. Wasn't that what mattered?

The only sound for long moments was the sound of the rain.

"You could have been killed," he said finally, still angry with her, still scared. "This was a stupid stunt."

"I got the photo." She stepped past him, head high, her wet leaf-strewn hair flipped to one side and her eyes bright with more than defiance. She was scared, too. She'd actually scared herself. Too bad she never learned from these kinds of experiences.

He watched her start up the road and swore under his breath, wishing she didn't do foolish things like this, wishing things were different between them, wishing she wasn't the only one who held out hope for the two of them, wishing he didn't want this woman so damned badly.

What was it his mother used to say? If wishes were horses, everyone would ride.

"Look," he said, going after her. Why did she always have to be so…Charity? But even as he thought it, he couldn't imagine her any other way. The thought surprised him, given how he felt about marriage and the mere mention of mixing their genes.

"Charity, I'm sorry I didn't—"

"—believe me?" she snapped.

"When I was looking for Nina's car, I was also keeping an eye out for your black pickup. If you'd just given me a chance—"

"You still don't believe the truck was following me, do you," she said, stopping in her tracks. "He left me another present. A rose. It was stuck to the passenger seat of my car when I left Betty's."

"I know. I saw it." Someone had put it in her car parked in front of the newspaper office while they were having a late lunch. The person had been that bold, and it scared the hell out of him. He wanted to be there the next time and catch the guy.

"You don't think it's the man in the black truck, do you." She shook her head as if disgusted with him. "Well, as soon as I develop this roll, you'll see."

He hoped so. "You have a photo of the driver?" He saw the flicker of uncertainty.

"You'll just see," she said, and continued up the road.

He pulled off his hat, raked his fingers through his damp hair, the rain feeling good on his face. "Get in. I'll give you a ride," he called after her.

She glared at him over her shoulder. It would be just like her to walk all the way back up the road in the rain to her car just to show him she didn't need him.

"Charity, come on. Let me give you a ride."

To his surprise, she stopped and came back to climb into the passenger side of the patrol car, although with obvious reluctance.

He got behind the wheel, found a wide spot to turn around and drove back up the road to her car, all the while trying to think of something to say. He was still angry with her. And she with him. Silence seemed safest.

The moment he slowed, she threw open the door and was out, headed for her car.

"Let me know when you get the photos developed," he said to her retreating back.

She didn't answer.

He waited until she turned the VW around, then followed her back down the road to the newspaper office. The blinds were up, the lights on inside the small building, and he could see her assistant, high-school student Blaine Bridges, inside working.

Charity parked out front and stomped into the newspaper office with her camera bag. She didn't give Mitch so much as a sideways glance.

He waited until she was safely inside before he drove down to his office. While he wasn't about to tell Charity, a photo of the pickup wasn't going to prove that the driver had been following her—or leaving her any presents. Neither would a shot of the driver. Even if the driver had left her the heart-shaped stone and the rose, there was no law against it.

The photograph she'd just risked her damned life for was worth nothing. All it would prove was that there was a black pickup in town with tinted windows and someone driving it.

But it *might* give Mitch a face, a license number, maybe, and possibly a name. And maybe a reason— if the truck really had been following her.

He left the patrol car and started through the rain toward Town Hall, where the Sheriff's Department shared the right half of the building.

A thought struck him. What had made Charity so sure the pickup was following her in the first place? Did she have some reason she hadn't told him about? Was she involved in something he was unaware of? What was the chance of that? Ha. About the same as the chance of rain.

What worried him was the possibility that it had something to do with Nina's disappearance and the questions Charity had been asking about her. But then, there was that damned baby spoon he'd found in Nina's bungalow. If Nina had been planning to blow the whistle on someone in town, then using Charity and the newspaper would be the best way to do it.

"Well?" Sissy demanded as Mitch walked into the Sheriff's Department office shaking off raindrops. She had that What's-Charity-done-now? look on her face.

"Do you know anyone who drives a black pickup with tinted windows?" he asked.

Sissy narrowed her eyes. "Not anyone in Timber Falls."

He nodded and walked into his office.

"Wade Dennison called. Wants an update," Sissy hollered after him. "Said you were to call the moment you walked in the—"

The last word was cut off as Mitch closed his office door. Damn Charity. He didn't want to admit just how much she'd scared him. He hung up his coat and sat down, still shaken.

He scrubbed his hands over his face, elbows on his desk. Maybe he *didn't* take Charity seriously enough. Except for her determination to get him to the altar. He took that damned seriously.

His intercom buzzed and he groaned. Surely Charity hadn't had enough time to develop the film already. "Yes?"

"Wade Dennison on line one. I told him you were heading for your desk as he called. You *owe* me."

There were too many women in his life, Mitch thought as he picked up line one. "Hello, Wade."

"What have you found out?"

Just enough to give myself a headache. "I've been looking for Nina, asking everyone who knew her where she might be, searching for her car. So far—" he hated to admit this "—I haven't turned up much."

"She didn't just vanish!" Wade snapped, then let out an irritated sigh.

"These kinds of investigations take time," Mitch said.

"Every hour that goes by is time lost."

"I know that, but in big cities, law enforcement doesn't even start a search until the person has been missing for at least forty-eight hours."

"This is not a big city," Wade said.

"No, it isn't, and that's why I've been looking for her and will continue looking for her. Wade, my other line's going. I gotta answer. I'll get back to you."

Mitch disconnected, shaking his head. Wade had sounded even more upset than he had earlier. What the hell had Wade's relationship been with the woman who called herself Nina Monroe?

Tracy Shank at Dennison Ducks thought Nina had something on Wade. Blackmail?

But people being blackmailed rarely got upset when the blackmailer suddenly disappeared.

Was it possible Wade and Nina had been romantically involved and that was why he was so upset?

That just didn't feel right to Mitch, either.

Maybe Wade had found out about the woman's lies.

But then Wade wouldn't have come to Mitch pretending he didn't know anything about her, would he?

And there was that damned spoon, Mitch thought, remembering it in his jacket pocket.

If Nina Monroe was Angela Dennison, then that would certainly explain a lot of things—like Wade's odd behavior. But Mitch couldn't see Wade keeping something like that a secret. Quite the opposite. Unless there was some reason Wade wouldn't want anyone to know that Angela had been found.

Mitch's head was killing him. He reached into his drawer, took out the bottle of aspirin, spilled two into his hand and downed them with the cold coffee in his mug on the desk. He shuddered at the bitter taste.

His door opened. "I'm leaving," Sissy announced as if she thought he might argue with her. "It's after five."

He glanced at the clock, surprised how quickly the day had gone. He'd hoped to find Nina before the day was out. He still had until midnight, but it would be dark soon, which would only make searching for her car more difficult.

"Have a nice evening," he said to Sissy.

She stayed in the doorway. "Are you all right?"

"Why?"

"You don't even have anything smart to say to me before I leave?" Sissy sounded disappointed.

"I used it all up on Charity."

Sissy laughed. "Good night, boss."

CHARITY COULDN'T WAIT to see what she'd gotten on film. She'd headed straight for the darkroom with her camera bag.

"Want anything from Betty's?" Blaine had asked. "I was just going to get some dinner."

"No thanks. I had a late lunch." Not even food could distract her right now. Once she had the roll of film developed…well, that was another story. "Take your time. I won't need you for a while." Right now she just had to see what she'd shot, and she didn't want any distractions.

"I'll return all those books to the shelves when I come back." A huge stack of books was sitting on the floor near the door to the storage room. Blaine had insisted on putting the books in alphabetical order by author. The boy just couldn't help himself.

As Blaine left, he locked the door behind him, and Charity stepped into the darkroom, shed her ripped-up raincoat and pulled her camera from the bag.

She was chilled to the bone, clothes drenched, teeth chattering. Her fingers shook as she tried to remove the film—and finally gave up. She kept an old sweatshirt and a pair of jeans at the office for "grunge" work. She stripped and changed into the dry clothing, including her favorite old red sneakers, then removed the film and began the developing process.

Most newspapers had gone to digital cameras, but she liked the old-fashioned darkroom process. There was something much more satisfying about it. But right now she would have loved to just zap the photos into a computer and see what she had.

The strip of negatives came out of the processor and she hung it up to dry. There looked to be a great shot of the front of the pickup and quite possibly the driver, although he was in shadow.

The same went for the dark furry animal that had run in front of the truck. It was only a blur off to one side, but it appeared to be nothing more than a bear. No Bigfoot.

However, there was good light on the front of the pickup. In fact, she could make out the last four figures of the license plate—4 AKS. She couldn't wait to take a closer look when the negatives finally dried and she could blow up the shot.

From what she'd seen quickly scanning the strip of negatives, she had all the shots she needed for this week's paper. Shots of Frank, the Granny's bread deliveryman, standing by the road where he'd reportedly seen Bigfoot looked as if it would work for page one.

She was thinking about how she'd lay out the page when she heard a thump outside the darkroom door. She turned, frowning.

"Did you forget something?" she called out,

knowing it had to be Blaine. The doors were locked and he was the only one with a key.

No answer. He must have already left again.

It had almost sounded as if he'd collided with one of the desks, she thought. What was he doing?

Another soft thump, this one closer to the darkroom. She froze as the knob on the darkroom door began to turn. The light was still on outside and Blaine knew better than to open the door while she was developing film.

The door opened. But even before she glimpsed the face distorted by a nylon stocking, she knew it wasn't Blaine.

MITCH GLANCED at the clock, surprised by how much time had passed. Even more surprised Charity hadn't called. She would have had the film developed by now. Maybe she hadn't gotten a clear shot of the pickup, after all. He couldn't imagine any other reason she wouldn't have contacted him otherwise.

He got up from his desk, stretched and realized he was hungry. That meant Charity must be starving. Maybe he could make amends by taking her to Betty's. The special tonight was stuffed pork chops, mashed potatoes with gravy, applesauce and double chocolate cake.

He got his coat and headed out the door, locking it behind him. The rain had let up. Temporarily. Fog hovered over the town like a bad omen.

As he walked down the block, he was unable to shake his uneasiness. Charity worked too many late nights at the newspaper. It was the nature of the business, but still, he didn't like her being there alone so often. Why couldn't that woman have gotten a normal job?

But as hard as he tried, he couldn't imagine Charity doing anything else. As a reporter she got to butt into people's business—and get paid for it. Journalism was obviously her true calling.

The blinds were drawn and the newspaper office was dark except for two faint lights he could make out through a crack in the blinds at the back of the building. A small glow to the left and the red light outside the darkroom across from it.

He couldn't see either Charity or Blaine. Was Charity still in the darkroom developing the film? Or had she gone to Betty's for dinner? The thought surprised—and worried—him. Charity had been so excited about what she was sure would be on the film. She wouldn't have left. That meant she had to be blowing up the photos in the darkroom now. Playing detective. Now that sounded like Charity.

He tried the front door. Locked. He knocked, waited, knocked harder. No answer. The newspaper was housed in a small narrow one-story brick building on a corner. Next door was a T-shirt shop that was closed. Behind it was an empty lot, overgrown with encroaching vegetation, a dirt alley separating the two.

As he walked around to the rear of the building, he was surprised how dark it was back there. Charity needed some sort of security light. He'd mention that to her, for all the good it would do.

As he neared the back, he saw that the door was ajar, a sliver of light spilling out onto the ground.

Maybe Charity had left the door open for some reason. He stepped closer and saw the telltale marks. The lock had been jimmied.

Heart in his throat, he drew his weapon and pushed open the door with his foot as he slipped through. The single light glowing off to the right was coming from the bathroom. It was empty, just like the office appeared to be. He moved to the darkroom door. The door opened at the turn of the knob and he caught a glimpse of something red on the floor just inside the door.

His blood thrummed in his ears. The darkroom was empty. Except for one of Charity's red sneakers, the white laces still tied, lying on its side on the floor.

Chapter Eight

Charity. Mitch's stomach cramped with fear as he took in her wet clothing hanging over a rod in the corner of the darkroom, and below them, the shoes she'd been wearing when she'd chased the black pickup.

There were empty film canisters scattered on the darkroom floor, and the contents of the camera bag was strewn over the counter. But no negative strips had been hung to dry. No photos pinned overhead.

He turned and moved through the small office: the layout area, photo light table, three desks, a copy machine in the corner.

In only a few seconds, he took it all in. The in-mail box turned upside down on the first desk. All the mail spread across the desktop, some on the floor, as if someone had gone through it. All three desktops a mess. The drawers open, contents obviously searched.

Like Nina's apartment. The burglar had been looking for something in particular.

But where was Charity? She would have been in

the darkroom working. She wouldn't have heard anyone at the back door. Or heard anyone come in... until it was too late.

Mitch felt sick. Was it possible the burglar had taken Charity with him? A terrifying thought.

He froze, listening. He thought he heard something.

There it was again. A muffled moan. It seemed to be coming from behind a bank of reference books stacked in the corner. It looked as if someone had been cleaning off the bookcase against the wall and been interrupted.

On the other side of the stack of books, Mitch spotted a door. This had to lead to a storage area of some kind.

Silently he moved toward it, aware that the intruders could be inside there with a knife to Charity's throat.

At the door, he stopped, listened. Another soft moan. The burglar could have his hand over Charity's mouth. Mitch tried to imagine that scenario and couldn't. Charity wouldn't have stood still for that. Especially if she thought someone was outside the door looking for her.

Mitch reached for the doorknob and turned it as quietly as possible. Locked. Another muffled moan.

He looked around for something to break the lock. A large petrified-wood paperweight sat on a nearby desk. He took it in one hand, his weapon in the other, and prayed as he brought the paperweight down hard on the doorknob. The metal knob thumped to the floor.

He jerked the door open, weapon ready.

It was pitch-black inside what was indeed a small storage closet. He could make out boxes of paper stacked high in the tight quarters. No room for a man to be holding a woman.

Fumbling, he found the light switch, flipped it and blinked as a bright bulb came on overhead.

For a moment, he didn't see her. Bound with wrapping tape, Charity was wedged in the corner between the stacks of paper boxes.

She blinked, blinded for an instant by the light. He saw relief swell in her brown eyes, but it was nothing compared to his. She made another muffled sound as she tried to speak through the tape over her lips.

He reached in and grabbed an end of the tape, jerking it off quickly to lessen the pain.

She let out a cry, but it sounded more like frustration and fear than real pain.

"Are you all right?" he asked as he moved a few of the boxes to get her out of her prison. Then he lifted her out and set her down gently on her feet. Her hands were bound with tape behind her, her ankles also wrapped tightly. She was fully clothed except for the one sneaker and didn't seem to be bleeding or injured as far as he could tell.

With his pocketknife he cut the tape, freeing her ankles and wrists. She wriggled as if to get the blood flowing again to her extremities, but he could see that she was trembling.

"Charity?" he asked, worried about her since she hadn't said a word yet and she'd seemed so anxious to have the tape off her mouth. He'd expected her to be talking a mile a minute. It scared him when she didn't.

He lifted her chin with his finger to look into her eyes and saw the unshed tears glittering there. She was shaking, her teeth chattering. He'd never seen her this frightened. Not even earlier when she'd scared herself falling down a mountainside in pursuit of a black pickup.

He drew her into his arms and held her tightly. "It's okay," he whispered against her hair. "You're fine." She smelled like paper stock.

She nodded against his chest and took several big gulps of air before pulling back to look at him. She seemed as if she was about to say something. Her lips puckered and several tears spilled soundlessly down one cheek.

Kissing her right then seemed as natural as breathing. He cupped her face in his palms. Her pulse jumped under his fingertips. He dropped his mouth to hers, wanting to kiss away all her hurt and fear. Wanting desperately to assure himself she really was all right.

Her mouth was pure nectar. Her lips parted, opening to him like a flower to a bee. He pulled her closer and deepened the kiss, his blood thundering in his ears.

At first she felt small and fragile in his arms. But soon his body became acutely aware of her wonderfully lush curves. Charity was all woman, rounded in all the right places. He felt that familiar and yet always shocking chemistry fire through him, warming him to his toes.

Her arms came up to loop around his neck. She pulled him more deeply into the kiss. Yes, she was just fine.

Her kiss was a potent elixir, as addictive as any drug, and he couldn't get enough of her. Oh, how he'd missed kissing her, holding her. He could never get enough of her. Never.

He felt dizzy and off balance and then, suddenly, he was falling. Dropping like dead weight off a bottomless cliff. Completely out of control.

He jerked back, disengaging his lips from hers. It always ended like this. With that horrible sensation of falling helplessly whenever he got too close to her. Even in his dreams at night about her. He would bolt upright in bed, heart pounding, and realize he'd just had a close call.

He felt that way right now as he cleared his throat and unhooked her arms from around her neck to hold her at arm's length.

Disappointment flickered across her features, then amusement, as if she thought him a fool for fighting the chemistry between them, because he could never win. It scared the hell out of him that she might be right.

He breathed deeply, trying to restore his equilibrium. ''Sorry about that. I just wanted to see if you were all right.''

"Uh-huh." Charity licked her lips, the kiss still lingering there, and grinned. He didn't really expect her to believe that, did he? "So am I all right?"

"Fine." He stepped back. Did he really think putting distance between them was going to help?

She'd seen how frightened he'd been and how relieved to find her. And that kiss...that kiss was no mistake. It was one honest-to-goodness kiss. She was trembling, but it had nothing to do with the intruder now.

But she could see from Mitch's expression that he was afraid the kiss would give her the wrong idea. He didn't want her to think that he might want her as badly as she did him. Or that he was finally coming around or that it was just a matter of time before she got him to the altar.

"It was just a kiss," she said. Uh-huh.

"Right." But he gave her a funny look as if to say the kiss had been a hell of a lot more than that.

Her head began to clear as she glanced toward the darkroom. "The bastard took the negatives, didn't he." She stormed past Mitch. She heard him swear under his breath, then follow her.

"You saw him?" Mitch asked.

She shook her head. "He was wearing a nylon stocking over his head. But I did get in one good kick." She glanced over her shoulder at Mitch. "From the sound he made, he was definitely male."

Mitch winced. Who said he didn't have a good imagination? "Did you see what was on the negatives before he took them?"

Again she had to shake her head. "But it *was* on there. The truck and maybe the driver."

"I should have believed you about the truck. I should also have come back here with you to develop the film."

"You can't protect me 24/7. Anyway, I never expected the guy to break in. I'm glad Blaine wasn't here." Who knows what that fool kid would have done. Or her burglar.

"Where *is* Blaine?"

She glanced at her watch. "He should have been back by now. Oh, Mitch, you don't think—"

"Where did he go?"

"To Betty's to get some food."

"Stay here," Mitch ordered. "Lock the door behind me and put a chair against the back door." He had his no-arguments face on. "I'll be right back."

She nodded, worried about Blaine.

Mitch was good as his word. "Blaine's fine," he said when she opened the door and let him in again a few minutes later. "Someone jumped him just this side of Betty's. He was bound up with tape in the alley. I sent him home to his mother."

"You're sure he's all right?"

"He's fine. His ego's a little battered, but he wasn't hurt. He was worried about you." Mitch held up his hand. "I told him you were fine. I didn't get into what happened."

She sighed with relief. Blaine was a sweet kid. She didn't want him worrying. Nor did she want this all over town—everyone knew what a gossip his mother,

Sarah, was. "I did see something on the negatives. Part of the truck's license plate number 4AKS. Sorry, that's all I got."

"Coupled with a description of the pickup, that might be enough to narrow it down," Mitch said, sounding excited. "You think it was the man driving the black pickup who broke in?"

"Who else?" She hadn't even been sure the driver of the black pickup had realized she'd taken his photo. He'd been busy trying to keep from hitting the furry beast that had crossed the road in front of his truck—probably a large bear. And she'd been well behind the animal when she'd taken the shots.

The driver must have seen her, though. He'd stopped his truck and looked down over the edge of the road—until he heard Mitch calling for her. Then he'd taken off fast. Which he wouldn't have done if he'd been looking down the mountainside for the bear. Or Bigfoot. Right?

So the burglar had to be the driver of the black truck. He'd seen her taking pictures and he'd come after the film. He must really not want her to know who he was.

"You're sure the back door was locked?" Mitch asked.

She nodded.

"It doesn't look like a professional job."

That was supposed to make her feel better? She'd had the truck, possibly even the driver's face on film. She might have been able to make an identification once she'd blown up the shot and maybe, just maybe, a blurred shot of Bigfoot. Or a large bear. Now she would never know. Now that she wasn't afraid, she was mad.

"What else was on that roll?"

"Just all the photographs I'd taken for this week's edition." She had to fight back tears of anger and frustration. She'd have to reshoot all of her lead photos. That meant the paper would be late this week. Some journalist she was.

"I'm sorry," Mitch said behind her.

She turned to face him. He *looked* sorry. He also looked worried. And it was obvious he didn't know what to say. Men. Right now would have been a great time to kiss her again and tell her he loved her. Even telling her he liked her a little would help.

"I can try to get fingerprints—"

"He wore gloves."

Mitch nodded and shifted his feet. Any hope of him declaring his love was quickly slipping away, along with any chance that he would kiss her again. He looked like a man who was dying to get away. Nothing new there.

"How long will it take you to figure out what was stolen?" he asked.

She shook her head as she looked at the mess the burglar had made on the desks. "My latest strip of negatives for starters." She suspected that's what he was after. So why ransack the office? Had he been looking for something else? Or had he just wanted her to think he had?

Mitch was staring at her, that lawman look on his handsome face.

She felt a prickle of worry.

"I don't want you going to your house alone tonight," he said.

Music to her ears. She smiled. "So what did you have in mind?"

He pulled out his cell phone and she watched him start to tap in a number.

"What are you doing?" she asked, afraid she already knew.

"I'm calling your aunt Florie."

"You wouldn't!" She grabbed for the cell phone, but he was too quick for her as he pulled it back out of her reach.

"Charity, I'd feel a whole lot better if you were at your aunt's tonight."

"Maybe *you'd* feel better…"

"Come on, one night. How bad can it be?"

Charity groaned, just imagining. "You live right next door to me. How much safer could I be?"

He was shaking his head, still dialing. "Or I can call your mother."

The ultimate threat. "Just shoot me now." Her mother would go ballistic, then load up the van with her commune family and drive into town with a plan to take her back to the farm. No way.

"Or I can lock you up in jail for your own protection. Sissy always comes in early. Her face will be the first thing you see in the morning and her voice the first thing you hear."

"You wouldn't." The only face Charity wanted to see first thing in the morning was Mitch's. But that offer didn't appear to be forthcoming.

She started to argue that she would be perfectly safe at home, the thief had gotten what he wanted, so why come after her again? But perusing the office, she wasn't sure that was true. Could the burglar be the same person who'd attacked her outside the post office, followed her and left her presents?

Also, she could see the determined set of Mitch's stubbled jaw and the pure steel in those wonderful blue eyes of his. He'd make good on *one* of his threats. She was trying to figure out which was the least of the three evils when she had one of her inspired ideas.

"What about my cat?" she demanded. "I have to be home to feed him."

"You have a cat?" Mitch asked, surprised.

Didn't every old maid? After all, at twenty-six, she was on the downhill slide to thirty.

Mitch was frowning. "Why can't I see you with a cat? What's his name?"

His name? "Winky."

"Winky?"

"Winky hates being left alone at night, and you'll be right next door if I need you," she said. "I can just yell." She picked up her purse from the floor, shoving everything back inside it. As far as she could tell, nothing was missing. Not even her twelve dollars in cash.

His frown deepened. He hit the last several numbers he'd been dialing. "Florie," he said, his gaze meeting Charity's glare. "Charity needs you to come stay with her tonight."

Charity crossed her fingers that Florie would be too busy telling Crystal from Evansville, Indiana, or Roberta from Spokane, Washington, about the position of her stars.

"Great!" Mitch said enthusiastically.

Damn. Her luck really stunk.

"Tell her not to bring the tarot cards," Charity said. But it was too late. Mitch had already hung up.

"She's meeting us at your house in five minutes."

Charity gave him her I'll-get-even-with-you-even-if-it-kills-me smile.

"Add it to that long list of things you'll never forgive me for," he suggested, as if she wouldn't. "I'll follow you home."

"You don't trust me to go by myself?"

"Not for an instant," he said, and motioned to the door. "I'll turn out the lights and lock up behind you. I suggest you get dead bolts installed tomorrow and a security light out back."

The man was impossible. And his lack of trust appalled her. But she did like his company and she *was* still shaken up. Not that she would admit it to Mitch. She couldn't stand the thought of him thinking she was one of those helpless females.

Aunt Florie came rushing into the house on a gust of wind only minutes later, her wizard-print caftan billowing around her small frame, her arms full.

"This really isn't necessary," Charity said, spotting what looked like one of her aunt's casseroles. Oh, no, this was going to be worse than she'd thought.

"It's no trouble at all," her aunt said. "I go where I'm needed." Florie charged into the kitchen and put her armload on the table, then threw her arms around Charity. "Tell me everything."

Mitch filled Florie in as Charity groaned inwardly, knowing her aunt was almost as bad as Sarah Bridges about spreading gossip.

"Oh, you must have been frightened out of your skin!" Florie cried, and hugged her again. "But not to worry. I'm here now. You'll be safe with me."

Mitch looked skeptical, but then, he did live next door.

"Where's your cat?" he asked looking around.

"He must be hiding," Charity said.

"You have a cat?" Florie asked.

"Winky?" Mitch called. "I don't see a litter box."

"He's trained to go in the toilet," Charity said.

"Really?"

"Why can't I see you with a cat?" Florie was saying.

Mitch carried Florie's huge suitcase upstairs to the guest bedroom. Charity caught him looking around for the cat. But Mitch was gone like a shot the moment Florie offered him some of the tofu-zucchini-eggplant casserole she'd taken out of the freezer for dinner.

"This person who broke in," Florie said as she

put the casserole in Charity's microwave when they were alone. "I don't like the vibrations I'm picking up. We'll have to consult the tarot."

Oh, damn, she *had* brought the tarot cards!

When Charity was younger, she'd gotten a kick out of Florie's predictions. Even Charity's best friend, Roz, loved to have her cards read. The two would stay up half the night laughing and talking about their futures.

Now, with thirty drawing ever closer, Charity would have preferred an aunt who didn't really "know" things.

At one time, Charity had believed her aunt really did know—right up until the point where the cards started suggesting Charity might not end up with Mitch.

"You know what I think? I'll bet your stars are out of whack," Florie said now, studying her through squinted eyes. "We must do your chart soon. I sense that trouble is brewing on your horizon."

Trouble was often brewing on her horizon.

Charity opted to take a hot shower while her aunt unpacked and the casserole nuked. The two-story house was small, with a nice-size living room decorated with furniture Charity had reupholstered herself.

She'd also done all the painting and put up the wallpaper in the kitchen and the tiny dining room. There was a half bath downstairs with a laundry room. She'd made a small room off the living room into a home office. Upstairs were two bedrooms and a bath.

Charity had bought the house because it was affordable, just the right size, on a quiet dead-end street at the edge of town and next door to Mitch's house. Theirs were the only two houses on that side of the block, with the town starting one street over.

"See, your aura is already improving," Florie said when Charity emerged a while later. Florie had her huge suitcase open. A flannel nightgown, a wooden baseball bat, candles and other paraphernalia, including a well-worn deck of tarot cards, covered the bed.

Florie hefted the baseball bat and smiled. "You're safe now, sweetie." What Florie lacked in stature, she more than made up for in attitude.

Mitch had always said that it was that indomitable attitude, along with a screwball wackiness, that was Charity's legacy. As if it was hereditary.

"Ready for dinner? You look like you could use a good meal."

Charity groaned. She *could* use a good meal and wished she'd conned Mitch into dinner at Betty's. She'd kill for a cheeseburger, loaded, a side of fries and a piece of pie.

"Don't look so worried," Florie said as she started down the stairs. "The cards will know what's going on in your life."

Which was why Charity hated the cards and this whole prediction thing. She couldn't stand the thought that her future was already written somewhere—especially if it didn't read the way she wanted it to.

"Where do you keep your cat food?" Florie called up from the kitchen. "I'll feed your cat."

"I don't have a cat," she called back.

"But I thought Mitch said—"

"What does Mitch know?" Charity pulled on jeans and a sweater for dinner, muttering under her breath, "I'm perfectly safe. Or at least I would have been without my aunt. If I get up to go to the bathroom tonight, she'll probably slug me with that damned bat."

She tried to convince herself that the thief had gotten what he'd broken in for at the newspaper. The negatives. But it still nagged at her that he'd taken the time to ransack her office. What had he been looking for? Something valuable to pawn?

No, she thought with certainty. He'd been looking for something in her mail—just as he had at the post office earlier when he'd knocked her down.

Chapter Nine

Mitch typed the partial license plate and description of the black pickup into the computer and crossed his fingers.

The match came up in a matter of minutes. A pickup with a license plate ending with 4AKS and matching Charity's description of the truck belonged to a Kyle L. Rogers Investigations of Portland.

Mitch checked the listing for Kyle L. Rogers Investigations in Portland and dialed the number. An answering machine picked up the call and informed him that Mr. Rogers was out of the office until next week. Mitch didn't leave a message. A private investigator?

He closed up the office and drove to Charity's.

She rushed to open the door in a pair of yellow-and-black penguin-print flannel pajamas. Her skin looked freshly scrubbed, a little flushed. Her hair was pulled up in a ponytail, the short curly hair at the nape of her neck still damp. And she smelled heavenly.

She threw herself into his arms excitedly.

It happened so fast he couldn't even be sure he initiated the kiss. Fortunately he disengaged himself from her lips as quickly as possible.

Her eyes were round as pie plates and she was smiling at him, that darned smile that said she'd get him to the altar yet.

"Don't just open the door to anyone who knocks," he chastised her, irritated with himself for kissing her.

She made a face. "Florie told me you were at the door."

"What did she do? Look in her crystal ball?" He knew why he was so annoyed. He was scared. Scared she was in danger. Scared she was getting to him.

"I saw your patrol car pull up," Florie said from upstairs.

He groaned inwardly.

"I have something important to tell you."

Charity looked as if she might pop. "You found the letter from Nina. I was right. The guy in the black pickup. That's why he knocked me down at the post office. That's why he broke into the newspaper and ransacked my office."

Mitch shook his head. "I did check your mailbox but there was no letter from Nina."

She looked disappointed but only for a moment. "But you have news. You found out who owns the pickup."

His expression must have given him away. *Was* Florie clairvoyant and *was* the ''gift'' in the Jenkins genes? It was a frightening thought.

"Yes, I do have a match on the pickup that was following you."

She looked as pleased as if he'd just slain a dragon for her.

"It's registered to Kyle L. Rogers Investigations out of Portland. Know him?"

She shook her head. "Should I?"

"Know any reason someone would put a private investigator on you?"

"No. You think someone up here hired him?"

Mitch thought about Charity's theory that Nina had not only written something down—she'd mailed it to Charity. Is that what Rogers was looking for? Then were was the letter?

He didn't know what to think. "Maybe. Maybe he's up here looking for Bigfoot."

He hoped knowing that the driver of the pickup was a private investigator would relieve her mind some. It had his. He didn't think this Rogers guy had come up here to harm Charity. Nor did he believe the P.I. was leaving her the presents. But he'd still be keeping a close eye on Charity tonight.

He moved toward the door. "If you see the truck again or need me…"

She nodded and smiled as she followed him to the door. "Glad you stopped by."

"Sure you don't want some vegetarian casserole?" Florie asked as she came downstairs.

"No thanks." He grimaced where only Charity could see.

"I will get you for this," she whispered, and then

he was gone out the door as fast as he could go. As he drove away, he saw Florie signal from the doorway that all was well with a baseball bat. Great.

As he drove down Main Street past the *Timber Falls Courier* office, he tried to concentrate, but he kept thinking about yellow-and-black penguin pajamas. And worrying that Charity wouldn't be safe, maybe especially with her aunt and that baseball bat.

He touched his tongue to his upper lip. He could still taste her, the feel of her mouth branded on his lips. What kind of fool was he to have kissed her? Not once, but twice today? It was the rainy season. It made people crazy.

He vowed once again to keep her at arm's length. Distance was the only thing that would save him. And even as he thought it, he wondered how the hell he'd ever be able to keep away from Charity—even if she'd let him.

As he passed the Duck-In Bar, he spotted Sheryl Bend's little blue car parked on the side. Earlier at the decoy plant he'd gotten the impression she'd wanted to talk, but feared retaliation from Wade.

He swung the patrol car into the lot, still hoping he'd find Nina Monroe before midnight.

As he pushed open the door, he wasn't surprised to see Sheryl sitting on her usual stool alone, staring down into her glass of beer. A country song played on the jukebox as he moved through the smoky din.

"Hey," Hank Bridges said as he slid a napkin in front of him. "What'll ya have, Sheriff?"

Sheryl swung her gaze from her beer to Mitch. She smiled, her eyes shiny with alcohol and invitation.

"A soda," Mitch told Frank, and pulled up a stool beside Sheryl.

"Haven't seen you in here in ages," she said, and took a sip of her beer, licking the foam from her lips.

He glanced around the bar, noting the regulars and a few faces he didn't recognize at several of the booths.

Out-of-towners were rare this time of year. Except when there'd been a Bigfoot sighting.

He turned back to the bar and Sheryl, glad he didn't see his father among the clientele. In the mirror behind the bar he caught the reflection of two people on the dance floor, both married, but not to each other.

That was another thing about the rainy season. It often led to affairs—and consequently divorces come spring. Former sheriff Hudson used to joke that Timber Falls held a roundup each spring to swap back wives and divide up the children.

"I wanted to talk to you," Mitch said to Sheryl after Hank slid an icy glass of cola in front of him and left. Mitch took a sip. He steered clear of alcohol. His father had drunk enough for both of them in his lifetime.

"Let me guess. You wanna talk about Nina," Sheryl said, sounding disappointed. "How come you never ask me out? How come you never take me up on dinner at my place?"

He smiled as he shook his head. He often wondered the same thing. But it seemed they both knew the answer.

"It's that damned Charity Jenkins, isn't it," she said.

He couldn't deny it. But he hadn't come here to talk about his love life. His nonexistent love life. "I got the feeling this morning talking to you that there was something you wanted to tell me about Nina but were maybe afraid to say anything with Wade up there…watching."

Sheryl sipped her beer, her eyes narrowing as she looked in the mirror over the back bar. "Nina was a back-stabbing bitch."

Mitch raised a brow. "Is that the beer talking?"

She swung her gaze to him. "That's the truth talking. The woman didn't care who she walked on to get what she wanted."

He took a wild guess. "She walked on you."

"She befriended me—just long enough to steal some of my duck designs, which she passed off as her own."

Mitch knew a little about painters at the plant getting royalties for new designs. "What did you do about it?"

"I went to Wade." She drained her glass and set it down a little too hard on the bar. Hank came over at once and twisted off the cap on another bottle of beer for her, sliding her a new frosted glass onto a fresh cocktail napkin before disappearing again down the bar.

"That son of a bitch Wade got mad at *me*. Said I

was trying to take credit for Nina's work and warned me if there was any more trouble I'd be put on notice." She narrowed her eyes at Mitch. "Do you believe that? I've been there ten years. Ten friggin' years. And that...bitch was there, what? A month?"

"How'd she get so close to Wade so quickly?" Mitch asked. Even if they had been romantically involved, it seemed damned sudden. Not to mention the age difference between the two.

Sheryl was shaking her head. "It was like maybe he'd known her before. I mean, he hired her just like that." She snapped her fingers. "Treated her like—" she waved a hand "—like he had to walk on eggshells around her. She had him by the you-know-whats." Sheryl sounded close to tears.

"Did Nina tell you anything about her past during the time you were friendly with each other?"

Sheryl shrugged and took a drink of her beer. "It wasn't for long, but she did mention an aunt once. Auntie Em. I swear to God that's what she called her. Like in *The Wizard of Oz*. She said she never knew her parents and couldn't stand her aunt."

"Sounds like she might have had a tough life," he said. The story could fit, if Nina Monroe was Angela Dennison—or wanted people to think she was.

"Probably every word of it was a lie." Sheryl took another long swallow of beer, licked the foam off her lips and stared down at the amber liquid miserably. "She still missing?"

"Yep."

"I hope to hell she stays that way."

Mitch had himself another suspect if Nina really had met with foul play, he thought as finished his soda. Now he hoped to leave before his father or Dennison Ducks production manager Bud Farnsworth showed up.

Unfortunately he was too late. Bud pushed through the door and they exchanged a look. Bud strode on past to the other end of the bar. That man was guilty of something, Mitch thought as he left.

In the patrol car again, Mitch cruised slowly by Charity's. All the lights were on, and through the thin curtains, he could see two figures sitting at the kitchen table. Just the thought of Charity eating tofu-zucchini-eggplant casserole brightened his mood.

He drove around town, making a loop by Florie's. Still no red compact parked in front of the Aries bungalow. He'd held out some hope that Nina had just bagged work and driven to Eugene for a day of shopping. If that was the case, then she had yet to return home. But it didn't explain the ransacked bungalow. Or Wade's anxiety.

The Ho Hum's No Vacancy light blinked bright red above the cars parked in front of the seven motel units. No black pickup. No compact. He wondered where Rogers might be staying. Probably down in Oakridge, twenty miles south.

At the *Courier* office, he checked the locks and windows. No one seemed to have come back. The town was quiet except for an occasional note or two drifting down from the jukebox at the Duck-In. Sheryl's car was still parked out front. So was Bud's pickup. Betty's Café was closed. Only the neon still glowed at the gas station.

Restless, Mitch drove out of town, not even realizing where he was going until he'd pulled the patrol car over to the side of the road and turned off his headlights.

The old place sat back from the road, the roof etched black against the trees. A light glowed inside, but he saw no movement. His father had probably taken off on foot through the woods to the Duck-In for his nightly drinking binge.

Just the sight of the house where Mitch had grown up made him aware of the painful void within him. He closed his eyes, trying to remember his mother's face, her voice, her touch, the part of his life he thought of as good, above reproach. Anything that would fill that awful hollow part of him.

But there was nothing of her left in him. It was spoiled by his bitterness toward his father.

Mitch opened his eyes and started to pull way. He shouldn't have come out here. Normally he avoided it at all costs.

But as his hand touched the gearshift, he saw him. A large dark silhouette against the light inside the house. His father stood at the edge of the covered porch, his huge hands gripping the rail, his head turned in Mitch's direction as if waiting.

Mitch shifted into first, snapped on the headlights, and got the patrol car moving. When he glanced back as he drove past, he saw that his father was still standing there, watching him run away just as he had watched Mitch's mother run away. Calling neither of them back.

AT FIRST IT WAS just part of the dream. The creak of a floorboard, the soft rustle of fabric, movement, then a deadly cold silence. It was the silence that dragged her up from dreamy sleep to wake to the terrifying knowledge that she was no longer alone.

Charity's eyes flew open. The blackness was complete—outside and in. No light anywhere. But she knew. Someone was standing just past the end of her bed. Realization stole the air from her lungs and sent her heart hammering.

She tried to convince herself it was just Aunt Florie. But the shape was too large, too solid. Too male. She couldn't see him, but she could feel him, hear him breathing, feel his gaze on her. How long had he been standing there watching her? The thought whizzed past in an instant of realization and horror, in the time it took her to breathe—and scream.

She lunged for the bedside table drawer where she kept her Derringer and pepper spray. The dark shadow at the end of her bed sprang to life. She thought he'd lunge at her, stop her before her hand could grasp the Derringer, swing and fire.

Her hand closed over the weapon. She swung. She hadn't heard his retreating footfalls over the percussion of her heart—or her scream. But she knew he was gone even before she heard the front door slam.

A light came on in the hallway. Her aunt appeared

silhouetted in the doorway in a long flannel night-gown gripping the baseball bat.

IT WAS NOT LONG after two, after the Duck-In had closed and Timber Falls resembled a ghost town, when Mitch went home. He'd driven around for hours and finally given up any hope of finding Nina or her car.

He heated himself a can of tomato soup and fell asleep fully clothed on the couch after making sure that everything next door seemed normal.

As usual, he dreamed of Charity. At first the scream was part of the dream.

He came awake with a jerk, knowing even before his feet hit the floor where the sound had come from. Diving out the door, he sprinted next door, weapon drawn.

When he reached the front steps, though, he froze at the sight of Florie with a baseball bat in her hands and Charity holding what looked like a gun. Both women were standing on the porch, looking scared—and scary.

"There was a man in the house!" Charity cried.

"Did you see which way he went?"

They both pointed across the street toward town.

"Get back inside. Lock the door. And put that gun away."

The street was empty. He took off running in the direction the women had indicated down a narrow alley. He hadn't gone far when he spotted a dark figure walking ahead of him. Not running. Just walking in long strides toward Main Street.

"Freeze!" Mitch leveled his weapon at the retreating back.

The man stopped but didn't turn around. He was tall, about Mitch's height, and strong-looking. He wore a biker's black leather jacket, jeans and biker boots.

Mitch moved quickly down the alley, keeping the weapon leveled at the man's back. "Put your hands behind your head." The light from a street lamp at the other end of the alley barely reached down here, so he still couldn't see who the man was.

Slowly, almost contemptuously, the man raised his hands, elbows out as he locked his fingers behind his head in a stance that was obviously familiar to him.

His hair was dark, long and pulled back into a ponytail. An earring glittered in his left lobe, and he wore a ring of thick gold on his right hand. It reflected the dim light as Mitch advanced.

But it was his stance that put Mitch on guard. He was used to bikers occasionally coming through town in the summer. Most were doctors or lawyers or computer whizzes, the kind of people who could afford a big motorcycle and the leather clothing that went with it, so there was never much trouble.

Seldom did Mitch see a biker this time of year. And this guy was no doctor or lawyer. Worse, there was something familiar about the way he moved.

"Turn around. Slowly," Mitch ordered, weapon still trained on him.

The man emitted a deep chuckle, then turned very, very slowly, grinning as he did. In the dim light, Mitch saw that his face was tanned and lean, his features strong. A woman, any woman, would have found him damned handsome. Many had. "Evenin', Sheriff."

Mitch had been right about one thing. This was no doctor. No lawyer. And certainly no computer whiz kid. Mitch shook his head and lowered his weapon. "Jesse."

"Hey, bro," Jesse Tanner said, dropping his arms and holding out his hand.

Mitch holstered his gun and reluctantly took his brother's hand. Jesse didn't seem to notice his reluctance as he threw his arms around him, slapping Mitch on the back. "Great to see you again, man."

Mitch stepped back from the embrace. It had been a long time and Jesse hadn't left under the best of circumstances. "What are you doing here?" he asked, telling himself it couldn't have been Jesse who'd been in Charity's house a few minutes ago.

"This is home, remember?"

"I remember you saying it would be a cold day in hell before you'd ever come back here," Mitch said.

Jesse shrugged and smiled, flexing those Tanner dimples. "People change."

Not Jesse, Mitch thought. Not his older brother, the hellion. "Someone just scared the living daylights out of Charity Jenkins. Were you in her house?"

His brother lifted a brow. "Already looking to bust me again?"

"You just happened to be in the neighborhood?"

"I was just seeing how much the town had changed." Jesse grinned. "It hasn't."

"Checking out the town at four in the morning?"

"I like the quiet."

Mitch stared at his brother, surprised how much he wanted to believe him. "How long have you been back?"

"Three days. I'm staying out at the house," he added, knowing that was going to be Mitch's next question.

He'd gotten back Saturday or Sunday? Odd that no one had mentioned seeing Jesse back after almost five years. Also, he was staying with their father.

"How *is* Charity, little brother?"

Mitch felt his stomach tighten.

"I hear she hasn't changed a damn bit. Still cute as a bug's ear and all spit and vinegar. She always was something. Too bad she's been hung up on the wrong brother for so long."

Mitch could remember all too well a time when Jesse had tried his best to steal Charity's heart—without any luck. Jesse had left town shortly after that—in handcuffs. He'd gotten into trouble with the law as usual, but Mitch remembered how upset Charity had been.

"So what are you driving now?" Mitch asked, thinking about the black pickup Charity thought had been following her.

"Got me a bike. A Harley."

"Know anyone who drives a black pickup?"

"I know a lot of people who drive black pickups."

"This one has dark-tinted windows."

Jesse seemed to think about that for a minute, then shook his head. "Doesn't ring any bells. Sorry."

Mitch couldn't be positive that the black pickup Charity had seen was Kyle L. Rogers's. She might not have gotten the plate number right. And mostly, he couldn't imagine his brother hiring a private detective to spy on her, but then, he'd never understood his brother. And the truth and Jesse seldom crossed paths.

"Someone in a black pickup's been following Charity, and the newspaper office was broken into earlier tonight," Mitch said.

He *could* imagine Jesse breaking into the newspaper to steal a strip of negatives. Jesse had left Timber Falls after being acquitted of burglary only because the old man had given Jesse an alibi that Mitch knew damned well was a lie but couldn't prove it.

But Mitch couldn't see his brother attacking Charity. If Jesse had wanted those negatives, he would have tried to sweet-talk Charity out of them. He wouldn't have had to bind her with tape and put her in a storage room.

Or maybe Mitch just didn't want to believe Jesse was capable of doing anything like that. Especially to Charity. "The thief locked Charity in a storage closet."

Jesse frowned. "Sounds like you got a regular

crime spree going on here. Any other unsolved crimes you'd like to pin on me?''

At least Jesse hadn't lost that chip on his shoulder, Mitch thought. ''I guess I'm just wondering what you're doing in Timber Falls.''

''Isn't it possible I got homesick?''

''No.''

Jesse laughed softly. ''I told you, bro, people change.''

But for the better?

''Okay, I'll level with you,'' Jesse said, and grinned. Like Mitch, he had the Tanner dimples. ''I was down in Mexico and I started thinking about Charity. I figured she was probably damned tired of carrying a torch for my brother by now, and I knew you sure as hell wouldn't have done anything like marry her, so I thought, Jesse, why don't you get on your bike and go see Charity? I thought she might want to run off with me.'' Jesse's laugh filled the alley. ''You don't have a problem with that, do you, little brother?''

Mitch gritted his teeth.

''I didn't think so,'' Jesse said. Then he sobered. ''I got homesick, Mitch. Plain and simple. I knew our old man wasn't getting any younger and I wasn't proud of the way I left things between you and me.'' His dark eyes were serious and he sounded so damned sincere. ''You should come out and see Dad. He'd like that.''

''But *I* wouldn't,'' Mitch said.

"Still carrying all that, are you?" Jesse shook his head. "It's been years, man. And he's changed."

"Yeah, everyone's changed. But I haven't."

"Maybe that's the problem." Jesse shook his head again. The grin returned. "Tell Charity hello for me. I won't kid you, man. I'm looking forward to seeing her." He turned and sauntered down the alley. "See ya 'round."

Mitch watched him stop in a deep shadow. The rumble of a big motorcycle echoed down the alley. A few seconds later Jesse roared off toward the place Mitch had once called home, the streetlight glaring off his helmet and shield, completely hiding his face.

Jesse was back in town, and just at the start of the rainy season. Mitch doubted it was because Jesse had gotten homesick, or that there was any chance Charity would just climb on the back of his bike and take off for parts unknown. She wouldn't, would she?

Mitch swore as he started toward her house. How *was* Charity going to take having Jesse back in town? Mitch hated to think that his brother could be right. Not that Mitch could blame Charity for getting tired of waiting around for him. But the last person he wanted to see Charity with was his brother!

Chapter Ten

Thursday, October 29

Charity awoke the next morning after hardly sleeping a wink all night. Mitch had come back and insisted on sleeping on the couch downstairs. Just knowing he was downstairs, only yards away, had made sleep impossible.

Worse, he'd come back in a horrible mood, hardly saying two words. He'd found a back window that had been broken into but no sign of the intruder except for some shuffled papers on her desk.

Maybe that was why he was so upset. He was obviously worried about her. She was starting to get worried herself. What had the person been looking for? A letter? That was the only thing that made any sense.

Charity realized she must have dozed off at some point toward daybreak because she awoke to the sound of pots and pans rattling in the kitchen below her bedroom. She jumped into the shower, made herself as presentable as possible and rushed downstairs.

Breakfast with Mitch would make eating whatever her aunt was cooking worth it.

"Where's Mitch?" she asked when she didn't see his lanky frame at the kitchen table.

"He was gone when I got up," Florie said. "He sure seemed in a foul mood last night, and I didn't like the look of his aura this morning one bit."

Just then the doorbell rang. Charity smiled, letting her imagination off its leash. She imagined Mitch standing on the porch, looking sheepish and apologetic, holding a bouquet of flowers—no, not flowers, a pie, a banana-cream pie from Betty's.

She swung open the door, her imagination so powerful she thought she could smell bananas.

Mitch wasn't standing on her porch.

And there was no pie.

"Jesse?" He was a darker version of his younger brother but had the same dimples. And right now his grin was all dimples.

Before she could utter another word, he dropped his bike helmet, picked her up and swung her around in a hug. "Damn, it's good to see you!" Still grinning, he set her down.

"What are you doing here?" His leather jacket was damp and cold with rain, and beyond him, she could see his motorcycle parked out front in the drizzling rain.

"I got lonesome for you," he said.

She ignored that. "Does Mitch know you're back in town?"

"Ran into him last night not far from here." He grinned again. "He didn't seem happy to see me."

"Not far from here?" she cried, latching on to his words. "You!" She swatted at him a couple of times in quick succession. "You were in my bedroom last night! It was you!"

He ducked out of her reach. "Whoa. If I'd been in your bedroom last night, you'd have damned well known it. In fact, I'd probably still be there this morning—" his grin broadened "—and so would you."

"Are you telling me you haven't been following me?"

He shook his head, the grin gone. "Mitch told me someone in a black pickup's been following you?"

She nodded. "Leaving me presents, too."

"Really?" He was grinning again.

"It *was* you!" She cuffed him again.

"Hey, you liked them, didn't you, sweetheart?"

"No, and don't call me that. What are you doing here?"

"I came back for you."

She stared at him. "No, seriously."

He flashed those Tanner dimples again, reminding her too much of Mitch. "Run away with me."

"Are you high on something?"

He laughed. "I just drove two thousand miles to see you. The least you could do is invite me in."

"I'm not sure you haven't already *been* in," she said, eyeing him suspiciously. But she moved back to allow him entrance.

"I've missed you like crazy, Charity," he said as he stepped into her living room. "I've even missed Timber Falls and Mitch. Can you believe it?"

"No," Charity said, closing the door.

"Jesse Tanner?" Aunt Florie cried from the kitchen doorway, a wire whisk in her hand.

"Florie!" In two strides, Jesse reached her, picked her up and swung her around, making her squeal.

Her cheeks were flushed and her eyes were shiny when he put her back down. "You're a sight for sore eyes, young man." Jesse had always been Florie's favorite.

"It's nice that *some*one is happy to have me back," he said, shooting a glance at Charity.

"I was just whipping up breakfast," Florie said. "Come have some with us."

Charity could not imagine what her aunt had whipped up.

"I'd love to have breakfast with you," Jesse said. "That is, if Charity doesn't mind." He gave her a wink.

"Not in the least." She was already reaching for her purse and car keys. "Wish I could stay, but I have to get to work," she said over her aunt's protests as she backed toward the front door.

She left Florie and Jesse and headed toward the newspaper office, which she drove right past when she saw Mitch's patrol car parked in front of Betty's.

MITCH WAS SITTING at the counter in his usual spot when Charity stormed in. She marched over and sat down on the stool next to him.

Too busy to stop and talk, Betty set a diet cola in front of her, a fork and a piece of butterscotch-cream pie, then bustled off.

"Why didn't you tell me Jesse was back in town?" Charity demanded, keeping her voice down.

Mitch looked over at her, pretending surprise that she was next to him. "Good morning to you, too. How do you know about Jesse?" He took a sip of his coffee as if his brother being back wasn't big news.

"He came by for breakfast."

Mitch cursed under his breath. "I figured you'd find out soon enough, since he says he's here because of you."

"And you believe him?"

Mitch looked over at her again. "Don't you?"

She made a face at him. "Some professional investigator you are." She took a sip of her diet cola. It calmed her a little. "He's been leaving the presents."

"He admitted that?"

She nodded. "And I think he was in my room last night, though he denies it. I just felt a presence there, looking at me in the dark."

Mitch stared at her. "But you can't be sure."

She shook her head.

"One of your back windows had been jimmied open," Mitch said and frowned, obviously thinking the same thing she was.

"Why would Jesse break into my house?"

"Why does Jesse do half the things he does?"

"Did he say how long he's been back in town?"

"Three days."

"So what's he been doing? Hiding out? Or hiding behind tinted pickup windows and keeping to the cover of darkness?"

"You make him sound like a vampire," Mitch said. "He's been staying out at the old man's."

Charity raised a brow. "And until last night, no one had seen him?"

Mitch rolled his eyes. Charity could be so dramatic. But she had a point. In a town the size of Timber Falls, news of Jesse's being back would have spread faster than a wildfire. Yet, other than their father, Mitch had been the first to see him last night. Or maybe Charity, if it really had been Jesse in her room. Sneaking into Charity's bedroom, though, sounded very unlike Jesse.

"Well, it definitely wasn't Jesse who broke into the newspaper office. He had no reason to want the negatives," she said. "But his timing bothers me."

Mitch couldn't agree more. After five years away, Jesse had come back to town the night before Nina Monroe disappeared and Charity had seen the black pickup following her.

He watched Charity take a bite of pie and close her eyes, savoring it. A small smile curled her irresistible lips. She opened her eyes and looked right at him, a satisfied gleam in her eyes that made him nervous, as if she knew something he didn't.

Normally one of his greatest pleasures was watching her eat since that was the *only* pleasure the two of them shared, but this morning he had other things on his mind.

Her eyes met his. He looked into those warm honey-brown depths and felt his body leaning of its own accord toward her. He could already taste her mouth on his.

The café phone rang. "It's for you, Sheriff," Betty called.

He blinked and jerked back. Charity had that damned knowing look on her face again. He got up and walked stiffly to the phone, afraid of who'd tracked him down at Betty's. He had a pretty good idea, but maybe it would be good news. Like Nina Monroe had shown up for work today.

"HOW'S THE PIE?" Betty asked, coming up to lean against the counter. It was obvious from her expression that she had some good gossip.

"Amazing," Charity said, and watched Mitch on the phone across the room. He'd almost kissed her, she was positive. "I think I like butterscotch pie better than banana-cream." When she'd taken a bite, she'd seen it, clear as day. Mitch in a tux standing beside her at the altar.

"What's this I hear about the paper being broken into and you being hog-tied?" Betty asked.

"Where did you hear *that?*"

"Twila told me that Kinsey told her that Shirley

told her that Lydia told her after Florie told her,'' Betty said.

Charity groaned. "Florie." Sure as the devil Mitch would think it was her fault Florie had blabbed.

In truth, she did blame herself. She'd let Mitch see how frightened she'd been. Big mistake. Now he'd want Florie to stay with her until this thing with the black pickup was resolved.

Not that she wasn't spooked by everything that had happened. Which was why from now on, or at least until she felt safe again, she'd be more careful—and carry her fear insurance with her. She had the small gun in her purse, along with the pepper spray and some handcuffs.

She'd also taken Mitch's advice and was having dead bolts and a back door security light installed at the newspaper office.

"So tell me *everything*," Betty said, salivating for the whole story. Charity could almost hear the hum of the grapevine. That was the problem with this town. No one ever waited for the paper to come out.

Charity stalled, took another bite of her pie and closed her eyes. All she saw this time was darkness, accompanied by the smell of cleaning supplies and newsprint. That damned storage room. It had freaked her out more than she wanted to admit.

She opened her eyes. Betty was waiting and Mitch was watching her from across the room.

"It's just like you heard," Charity confirmed, and added enough details to thrill Betty, then asked, "Did you hear if Nina Monroe's been found yet?" If anyone would know, Betty would. And probably sooner than Mitch.

"No one's seen hide nor hair of her," Betty said. "Odd, isn't it, and at the same time as a Bigfoot sighting." She hummed the theme from *The Twilight Zone.*

Charity groaned. "You aren't suggesting the two are somehow linked, are you?" Ridiculous. But it would make for a great headline: Bigfoot Abducts Local Duck Painter.

Betty leaned toward her. "Remember that little boy who disappeared in the Cascades south of Portland? Lost for days in the mountains. No one thought he'd be found alive, not with the temperature dropping at night and no food or water." She straightened and nodded. "And what happened?"

Charity knew the story. It was the fabric from which legends were woven. "They found the boy alive and well."

"And when they asked him how he'd managed," Betty said, finishing up the story with her I-told-you-so look, "he said a nice monster took care of him." She broke into *The Twilight Zone* theme song again. "Nina could do worse," she said, and took off with a pot of coffee in each hand.

Charity wondered if that was true, Nina doing worse than being abducted by Bigfoot.

The café was busy, what with the regulars and all the visitors the Bigfoot sighting had brought to town. The Halloween weekend ahead would be worse. Especially if there was another Bigfoot sighting.

Charity thought about the blur of brown fur she'd caught on film. Had it just been a big bear?

Losing those photos hurt worse than being bound and gagged and stuffed between boxes of paper in a storage closet. Almost. She had to reshoot and get the newspaper ready to go.

But this thing with Nina had become a better story than Bigfoot—unless the call Mitch had taken was someone telling him that Nina was no longer missing. And if the black truck that had been following her really was just some private eye…

But why had someone stolen her film? A chill skittered up her spine. There had to have been something incriminating on that roll of film. Something more incriminating than a photo of a black truck.

But who else would be interested in the photographs? She tried to remember everything that had been on that roll.

That's when it hit her. Nina Monroe. *She'd taken a photo of Nina.* And that wasn't even the worst of it. She remembered now who might have seen her do it.

HANGING UP the phone after listening to a resident rant and rave about a barking dog, Mitch returned to his pie and coffee—and Charity. He never dreamed he could get hooked on pie for breakfast, and all because of a woman. But he had to admit as he slid onto the stool next to her, pie beat the hell out of oatmeal.

Charity had ruined him for any other breakfast.

Just the way she'd apparently ruined him for any other woman, he thought grimly. Still, he couldn't believe he'd almost kissed her. Again. And in Betty's. And it was only the *beginning* of the rainy season. Hell, he could be married to Charity by spring the way he was going.

"Mitch," Charity said excitedly, "let's get out of here! There's something I have to tell you."

"Florie read something disturbing in your coffee grounds this morning?"

She pushed her pie away and stood.

Mitch looked from the unfinished butterscotch pie to Charity. "Are you sick?"

"Funny. My stars are out of alignment and there is trouble on my celestial and terrestrial planes. I won't even tell you what else the tarot cards had to say."

"Good." It was pouring rain outside, but he figured he was going to need the fresh air. He downed most of his coffee, left enough money for it and Charity's breakfast and a tip, grabbed his coat and hat, and followed her outside.

Rain drummed on the roof overhead and poured in a sheet off all but one side. He hunkered down in his fleece-lined county-issue jacket, chilled more by the look on Charity's face than the weather.

She took a breath and let it out on a puff of white. "The guy from the black truck might not have been the one who took the strip of negatives. I remembered who else I'd shot on that roll of film—Nina."

"*Nina?* You shot a photograph of Nina and you

just now remembered?'' Since Charity might have
had the *only* photograph of Nina, he found it hard to
believe she'd forgotten until now.

"Get in the patrol car," he ordered.

Charity couldn't believe it. "You're going to arrest
me?"

His look said it would be prudent if she got into
the patrol car without making a scene in front of
Betty's.

Good thinking.

She dashed through the rain to where the patrol car
was parked on Main Street and climbed in the passenger side as he slid behind the wheel.

Without a word he started the engine, but didn't
drive away. He turned on the heater. The windows
began to clear.

It was cozy in here, nice to be out of the cold and
wet. The rain made a pleasant sound on the roof, and
she could smell Mitch's subtle aftershave, along with
a warm maleness.

She breathed it in and closed her eyes, and for just
an instant, she saw herself dressed all in white and
next to her—

"Charity."

Her eyes flew open. "I'd forgotten I took a candid
shot of Nina when I was at Dennison Ducks. After I
talked to her about an interview I staked out the parking lot since I'd heard Wade often left right after
Nina at lunchtime."

"And?"

"She came out, but she didn't go to her car. She

walked toward the back of the building, stopped and was arguing with someone.''

''Did you see who?''

She shook her head. ''I couldn't hear the words, either. She had her back to me. But I could tell she was mad about something.''

''I'll take your word for it.''

''She stomped to her car, got in and drove off. I took a shot of her right before she took off.''

''That was it?''

''Not exactly. I ducked down behind the trees again, put my camera away and started back to where I'd left my car parked down the road and…I ran into Wade.''

Mitch let out a low whistle. ''Did he see you take Nina's photograph?''

''Maybe. He couldn't have been the person she was arguing with, though. He came from the wrong direction, *through* the trees.'' There was an old bridle path behind the plant that lead to town and the Dennison mansion.

''His car wasn't in the lot?''

She shook her head. ''I think Wade was spying on Nina.''

''It makes more sense than them having an affair.''

She chewed on a nail for a moment. ''You're going to think I'm crazy, but I have this theory.'' She could tell Mitch didn't want to hear it. ''Nina is the right age, the right coloring and given the way Wade treated her…'' She met his gaze. ''I think she's Angela.''

He tried to appear shocked, but he couldn't fool her. "Nina *is* Angela!"

"Whoa! I didn't say a word," he protested.

"You, as the most cynical person on earth, wouldn't think Nina was Angela unless...unless you had proof! You found proof?"

"Stop. You're impossible." He rubbed his forehead as if he had a headache.

"Oh, I love it when I'm right! Tell me. You have to tell me. That's why you've been so worried about me. You know something. But what does it have to do with me?"

"Charity, I don't know what it has to do with you. That's why I have to tell you. But it's strictly off the record. It could be evidence in a murder case."

She hated anything being off the record, but she was dying to know what he'd found out. "Fine."

He told her about the silver baby spoon he found in Nina's bungalow.

"It's Angela Dennison's?"

"Looks that way, but I need to show it to the jeweler in Eugene who made it before I'll know for sure."

This was better than she'd hoped and the possibilities made her head spin. "The kidnapper could have taken the spoon, Nina found it and was blackmailing the kidnapper."

"Why would the kidnapper take the spoon?"

She shrugged. "Could have seen it by the bed. Took it because it was solid silver. Or because it represented the Dennison's wealth."

He nodded. "You mean someone jealous of a baby born with a silver spoon in her mouth?"

She smiled. "Exactly. Since no ransom was ever demanded for Angela, he must have sold the baby or…been paid to take it." She could see that Mitch had already considered that possibility. "Or with the baby spoon, Nina could pass herself off as Angela. Or she really is Angela."

"The reason I told you about the baby spoon was so you'd understand how dangerous this could be. Especially for a nosy newspaperwoman who took a photo of Nina *one day* just before she disappeared."

"I wish I *had* that photo. Florie might be right about my stars being out of whack."

"I could have told you that without even looking at your stars." His gaze softened. He reached across the seat and took her hand, cupping it in his, sending a satisfying jolt through her. "I'm serious. I'm worried that you're in danger. I don't want you doing this story. At least not yet."

She was too lost in the feel of his warm fingers tracing over her skin to argue—at least for the moment.

A loud tap on the window behind Mitch's head made her jump.

Wade Dennison peered through the rain-streaked glass. He was looking past Mitch straight at her. "Charity Jenkins! You damn meddling woman," Wade bellowed. "I'm going to kill you!"

Chapter Eleven

Sissy shot Mitch a what-now look as he and Wade burst into the Sheriff's Department, raindrops puddling at their feet and Wade bellowing, "I want that woman locked up!"

It was clear Sissy knew what woman Wade was referring to and was in full agreement.

Mitch marched Wade into his office and closed the door.

"What the hell is Charity doing asking about Nina?" Wade demanded before the door closed. "Did you know she talked to some of my people? Asked a bunch of personal questions? You have to do something about her."

"Sit down, Wade." Wade didn't. Mitch walked around behind his desk and dropped into his chair, counting to ten before saying, "In the first place, Wade, I can't do anything about Charity because she hasn't broken any laws. But if you threaten to kill her again, you could end up behind bars. Being the local press, she has certain rights," he hurried on before Wade could argue. "Rights protected under the First Amendment."

"That allows her to butt into other people's business?" Wade demanded, slamming his fist down on the desk.

"Yes, actually, it does."

Wade slowly lowered himself into a chair. "The woman's a menace."

Mitch couldn't argue that. He was worried as hell about her. But he couldn't stop her from pursuing this story any more than he could get Wade Dennison to tell him the truth.

He studied the man across the desk from him. When Wade had shaved this morning, he'd missed a patch of gray whiskers on one side of his jaw, and his eyes were bloodshot, the skin under them baggy and dark as if he hadn't slept.

Still, Wade carried himself with an air that said he could make or break this town if he didn't get his way. In that sense alone Wade Dennison was dangerous.

What worried Mitch was the chance that Wade was more dangerous than any of them knew. He'd been in a rage outside Betty's a few minutes ago, threatening Charity. Mitch wondered if Wade was capable of violence and if Nina Monroe had been the first to find out. Or if Angela Dennison had been.

"Wade, it's time you told me what the hell is really going on."

CHARITY COULD almost feel her ears burning. She would have loved to know what was being said about her over at the Sheriff's Department.

But she had work to do. And it wasn't as if Mitch had invited her to tag along with him and Wade. She probably didn't want to hear it, anyway.

She couldn't believe Wade had actually threatened to kill her, and in front of the sheriff. Was it possible that Wade had been the man who'd broken into the newspaper, stolen her negatives and bound and gagged her in the storage room? Wade might be in his sixties, but he was strong as an ox, and even if he hadn't been wearing a nylon stocking over his head, she'd never gotten a good look at the man who'd attacked her. Nor at the one who'd been in her bedroom.

A few days ago, she would have scoffed at the idea of Wade Dennison as her assailant and intruder. But seeing Wade's rage this morning, she wasn't so sure. The man seemed out of control. And all because of Nina Monroe. Now why was that?

She drove to her office in time to pay the handyman who'd installed her dead bolts and a security light out back, then locked up and, using her ladybug umbrella, walked down Main Street to the Busy Bee antique shop.

She couldn't still her excitement. She'd only asked a couple of people she knew who worked out at Dennison Ducks about Nina, and now Wade was in a murderous rage. There was definitely a story there. Nina Monroe might actually *be* Angela Dennison.

But wouldn't Wade have been delighted to have Angela back? Wouldn't he have told everyone? His behavior didn't make any sense and made her all the more determined to find out what was going on.

A tiny bell tinkled as Charity pushed open the door to the antique shop and was instantly assaulted with the wonderful smell of antiques—and peppermint tea.

The Busy Bee was anything but busy. The owner, Lydia Abernathy, smiled and waved from the back. She was a tiny woman, her hair a white downy halo around her head, her blue eyes a bright twinkle in her wrinkled face.

"You're just in time for tea, dear, and I have your favorite sugar cookies."

"The ones with the sprinkles on top?" Charity asked as she made her way through the antiques to the back.

"Of course." Lydia zipped over to the hot plate in her motorized wheelchair to get the teapot. She already had another cup and saucer out.

"You must have known I'd be stopping by," Charity said, dragging up a chair.

Lydia laughed. "Yup. As soon as I heard about my brother's behavior outside Betty's this morning. Everyone in town heard Wade hollering." She clasped her hands together in obvious delight. "Do tell me what you did to tick Wade off."

WHEN MITCH GOT tired of Wade's threats and obvious avoidance of the truth, he gave up and asked him to leave.

Wade stood and seemed to hesitate. "I'm telling you I don't know what happened to Nina."

Mitch nodded impatiently. "Why don't you tell me why you're so protective of her?"

"I'm protective of all my people."

"Dammit, Wade, you didn't even check her references. She never worked at any of those places she put down on her application." Wade started to interrupt, but Mitch cut him off, raising his voice. "You didn't check her social security number, either, or any other identification. Her name isn't even Nina Monroe."

Mitch hadn't planned to tell Wade that. At least not yet. But now that he had, he waited for a reaction and wasn't surprised when Wade didn't even flinch. "So you already knew that. Okay. Who is she?"

Wade just looked at the floor and shook his head.

"Is there any chance the reason you're so upset is because the woman who called herself Nina Monroe is actually Angela Dennison?"

Wade's head snapped up. "That's ridiculous. You get that from that so-called reporter girlfriend of yours?"

Mitch could almost see Sissy straining to listen on the other side of the wall. "I asked you a question. Just answer it. Is there even a chance that Nina is Angela?"

"Hell, no."

"Hell, no, you won't answer. Or hell, no, she wasn't Angela?"

"Just plain hell, no." Wade stormed over to the door and flung it open. "Do your damned job. Find

Nina. I have to go out of town. I'll call you when I get back this evening.'' He slammed the front door on his way out.

Sissy stuck her head in the open doorway of Mitch's office as Wade's car roared away. "You want coffee? Colombian roast."

Sissy never got him coffee. Always said his legs worked just fine. So what was this about? Plain old nosiness, he decided. This town had more of it per capita than any town in the country, he'd swear. "No, and close the door."

"Ouch!" Sissy said, unperturbed as she shut the door.

Mitch tried to calm down, but couldn't. He unlocked his drawer and pulled out the Angela Dennison file again.

If someone in the house had abducted the baby and tried to make it look like a kidnapping, what would they have done with her? Killed her? Buried her in the backyard or the woods? Left her on a doorstep? Sold her?

Is that what he thought Wade had done? Gotten rid of Angela? And Nina had found out and was blackmailing him? Or Nina *was* Angela.

Mitch flipped through the interviews Sheriff Hudson had done after the abduction, fearing this old case was the key to Nina Monroe's disappearance. Jotted in the margins was a note. A name jumped out at him. He flipped back and stared down in disbelief. Ruth Anne Tanner. His mother? The sheriff had tried to reach Ruth Tanner to question her about her visit to the Dennison house earlier on the day of the kidnapping twenty-seven years ago?

"Where can I reach you?" Sissy asked as Mitch he stormed out.

"The Dennison house."

"Oh."

Mitch couldn't have been more shocked as he drove out of town. Why would his mother go to see Daisy—the woman who'd been having an affair with Ruth Tanner's husband?

Mitch tossed his hat on the seat beside him and raked his hand through his hair. His head ached and he couldn't shake the bad feeling at the pit of his stomach.

His mother had dropped by for a visit with Daisy? Not bloody likely. She must have gone over to the house to confront Daisy about the affair, demand Daisy leave her husband alone.

He'd only been six but he remembered that day like it was yesterday. He'd come home from school to find not only his mother gone, but all her things. She hadn't even left a note. She was just gone. He'd found his father sitting on the deck facing the road. He'd told Mitch that he didn't know why she'd left, but they'd both known. They'd never heard from her again.

Years later, Mitch had tried to find her but to no avail. She'd probably changed her name. She obviously didn't want to be found for she'd left no trail.

So what had happened at the Dennison's that day?

Had Daisy refused to break off the affair? Is that why his mother had left the way she had?

Mitch shook his head at his mother's timing. She had gone over to see Daisy just hours before the woman's baby was stolen—and before she herself disappeared without a trace.

The two couldn't have anything to do with each other. Dear God, he hoped not.

THE DENNISON HOUSE was pretentious at best, a huge plantation-style home with white pillars, porticos and a sweeping lawn completely out of place in the middle of the mountains of Oregon.

Out back was an indoor pool and recreation room. Beyond that, stables and corrals, where Daisy Dennison had once raised expensive horses.

Mitch parked the patrol car in the woods a couple of hundred yards from the house, checked his watch and waited, knowing there was no turning back once he knocked on the Dennisons' front door.

A few minutes later he saw the housekeeper leave. Anyone could have set a clock by her schedule. She drove into town the same time every day to do the shopping.

He figured Desiree would still be in bed this early, and Daisy would be forced to answer the door. He rang the bell a dozen times before she finally did.

She looked furious. He wasn't surprised, given their past. Or his persistence.

Her appearance, though, startled him, and he tried to remember the last time he'd seen her. She didn't come into town anymore, not that she'd ever embraced the locals. Most worked for her husband and so were beneath her.

Her implicit snobbery and her former legendary shopping trips to New York and Paris, among other things, had made Daisy Dennison the talk of Betty's for years. Back then, she'd dressed to kill, driven the most expensive cars, ridden the best horses money could buy and done whatever she damn well pleased, all the time rubbing it in everyone's faces, including her husband's.

That was until Angela's kidnapping. After that, Daisy had become a recluse, which started its own round of gossip. But even that had died down over the years, due to a lack of fresh dirt.

As far as Mitch knew, Daisy Dennison was seldom seen by anyone except her immediate family and their housekeeper, a tight-lipped German named Zinnia.

Zinnia did all the shopping, but spoke only broken English and didn't gossip, a crushing blow to Betty's crowd.

So Mitch was taken aback by how much Daisy had aged. Wade had shocked the town when he'd brought his new mystery bride home to Timber Falls. Daisy, a dark-haired beauty, was nineteen at the time, Wade forty. Great gossip down at Betty's for weeks.

Now Daisy, who wasn't even fifty, looked older than her husband, who was hugging seventy. She was far too thin. Her once gorgeous hair was dull and graying and pulled severely back from her face. Her clothing was equally stark—baggy black sweats and worn black slippers.

There was no color in her face, no light in her eyes, not like the way she'd looked the summers she'd ridden her horse on the trail behind his house. Mitch had been just a kid, but he still recalled his father disappearing into the woods on those sunlit mornings and coming back in the late afternoon smelling of wine and perfume.

Mitch shoved aside the memory the way he did most thoughts of his father. Always better not to go there.

"Mrs. Dennison. Sorry to bother you, but I'm working on a missing person's case and I need to ask you a few questions."

Her look berated him for not calling first.

But they both knew why he hadn't.

"It will only take a few minutes."

She glanced at her watch as if trying to come up with an excuse. She didn't need an excuse not to talk to him and they both knew it. With an irritated sigh, she stepped back and let him enter.

He wondered about her life as she led him into a large living room to one side of the house. Long windows ran the perimeter of the room on three sides, providing views of the front, side and back yards and the deep green of the encroaching wilderness beyond—if the blinds hadn't been closed. The room was as dark and gloomy as the weather outside and the woman in it.

What did Daisy Dennison do in this huge house

all day? And why had she closed herself up here all these years? He wondered what it must be like for her daughter Desiree, who still lived at home. Or maybe that was why Desiree stayed here—for her mother.

"What is it you want?" Daisy asked impatiently, motioning to a chair, making it clear he wouldn't be sitting long.

"One of the decoy painters is missing. Nina Monroe." He waited for a reaction and got none. Hadn't Wade told her about Nina? Obviously not. By just coming here, he was treading on thin ice. He decided to dive in and get it over with. "Wade is worried Nina might have met with foul play."

"I've no interest in the decoy business." Her tone made it clear she never had.

"Even if your husband and Nina have a relationship?"

The smile was bitter. "Especially if that's the case." She started to get up. "You should have called. I could have saved you the trip."

"Why did my mother come to see you the day Angela was abducted?"

Daisy Dennison lowered herself slowly back onto the chair, her face stony. "She wanted money to leave town. She thought she could blackmail me."

"That's a lie." The words were out before he could stop them.

She arched a brow. "You obviously didn't know your mother. How old were you—six when she left? I threw her out and never saw her again."

"What about my father? Did you see him again?"

Her gaze softened. "No. Not after I lost Angela. I doubt you'll believe this, either, but I loved your father."

He got to his feet. "I'd like a word with Desiree."

It was her first genuine emotion. Fear. "Desiree doesn't know about your father and me."

"But she might know about Nina Monroe," he said. Daisy couldn't keep him from talking to her, though she might try.

"Nothing can change the past," Daisy said, her voice sounding like an old woman's, weak and shaky, all that confidence and bravado gone. "Can't you leave it buried for all our sakes?"

"I wish I could, but I'm afraid some things just won't stay buried."

Her dark eyes glinted with tears. She walked to the back wall. He thought for a moment she was calling someone to have him thrown out.

But instead, the blinds on the windows there groaned upward. She pointed toward the indoor pool, then reached for the phone, dismissing him.

He listened to her dial. She was calling her husband, sure as hell. Wade would be furious. Not that it mattered. It had been more than thirty-six hours since Nina was last seen. Mitch couldn't shake the feeling he was now investigating a homicide.

"OH, THESE COOKIES," Charity moaned with pleasure.

"Better than sex?" Lydia asked with a wink.

"If I ever have sex, I'll let you know."

Lydia laughed, then leaned forward in her wheelchair. "So tell me. Why are my brother's shorts in a bunch over this decoy painter?"

"I was hoping you could tell *me*. No one seems to know anything about her. Have you ever seen Wade this crazy before?"

"Just once," the older woman said. "When Angela was taken."

Charity nodded, counting on that answer. "You remember anything about that time?" she asked as she took another cookie.

"Like it was yesterday," Lydia said.

WARM MIST rose off the turquoise-blue water to fog the glass windows. Through the mist, Mitch saw Desiree Dennison lying on a lounger by the pool wearing a pale-pink one-piece. The suit was wet, her tanned skin covered with tiny droplets of water, the room hot as a sauna.

She glanced up as he approached. She reminded him of a sixteen-year-old. Not only because she was young-looking, but because she acted young. He found it hard to believe she was three years older than Charity.

"Sheriff Tanner?" Desiree sounded surprised. Was it possible she hadn't heard Nina Monroe was missing? Or maybe she couldn't have cared less, just like her mother.

"Is there someplace less…damp we could talk?"

She groaned and covered her eyes with one slim

arm. "I have a bitch of a hangover and I'm in no mood for a lecture."

"I didn't come here to lecture you."

She lifted her arm and gazed up at him. "Did I break one of your laws?"

Probably a half dozen. "They aren't my laws. Would you mind putting something on?"

She looked down at her tanning-bed tanned full-figured body, then up at him and smiled teasingly. "Sure, Sheriff, if that's what you want."

He looked away as she slowly rose from the lounger and slipped into a large long-sleeved man's shirt. He wondered whose shirt it was. Definitely not her father's taste.

"Want something to drink?" she asked as she led him from the pool area into the game room, complete with dozens of commercial-size video games.

"Beer? Soda? Bottled water?" she asked as she went behind a bar and opened a small fridge.

"Nothing. Thanks."

She shrugged as she twisted the top off a bottle of beer, careful not to break her long lacquered nails.

"Come on, Daddy asked you to talk to me about…what? The evils of alcohol? Drugs? Speeding?" She grinned. "Sex?"

"I'm here about Nina Monroe's disappearance."

"Who?"

"The decoy painter at your father's plant everyone's talking about," he said patiently.

Desiree grinned. "I might have heard something

about her at the Duck-In last night, but why ask me about her?''

''You never met her?''

She wrinkled her nose. ''I don't hang out with people from the plant.''

''Never ran into her at the Duck-In?''

She shrugged. ''I guess not.''

''Your father thinks Nina might have met with foul play.''

''You mean like someone *murdered* her?'' She made it sound as if Timber Falls could never be *that* interesting. He wondered why she'd stayed here. Was it the pool, the stocked fridge, the free ride on Daddy's money? Or was she afraid to leave her mother alone in this big old house?

She took another drink.

''One more question,'' he said, tired of the Dennison women. ''What would happen if Angela came back?''

Desiree choked. ''The precious younger child I've never been able to live up to because I'm still *alive?*'' She made a disgusted sound. ''Why would you even ask that? You don't think Nina—''

''Just curious.''

She studied him for a moment, obviously battling with the idea. ''My parents would stone her to death because how could she possibly live up to the perfect lost child they've canonized for twenty-seven years?'' She looked at him, bitterness souring her gaze. ''But you know, even if she wasn't the perfect daughter, she'd still make me look bad, wouldn't she?''

Chapter Twelve

As Mitch drove away from the Dennison house, the radio squawked and Sissy came on.

"I think one of your Bigfoot fanatics might have found something you've been looking for," she said.

"Go to the security channel."

A moment later, "You there?"

"Go ahead."

"Just got an anonymous call from some guy who says he spotted an older red compact in a ravine. He says he thinks there's someone in the car. Too steep to go down there. He called to the person a few times, but got no answer. So he drove out to report it. Didn't want to get involved, so he declined to give a name. Called from the pay phone outside the Duck-In."

Mitch muttered an oath. Wasn't this what he'd feared all morning?

"Where'd he see the car?"

"Just past Lost Creek Falls."

Seven miles out of town. "I'm on my way." He reached Main Street and started south on the highway. No lights. No siren. Watching his speed. He didn't want to add to the rumors already whizzing around town.

Suddenly a figure in a bright-red rain slicker rushed out into the street, arms waving. All he caught was a flash of red before he hit the brakes. The patrol car skidded on the wet pavement, coming to a stop just inches short of catastrophe.

Charity grinned at him from under her hood and stepped around to the passenger side to open the door.

"Have you lost your mind? I almost hit you," he hollered, his voice betraying just how close he'd come. Wade was right. The woman was a menace.

"You would never run me over," she said as she calmly climbed in and buckled her seat belt. "You might want to—" there was a smile in her voice "—but you wouldn't."

"What do you think you're doing?" he asked.

"I thought you might want to have some lunch," she said. "Betty made coconut-cream pie and I've found out a few things you're going to want to hear, such as Wade and Daisy had a huge fight the night Angela disappeared."

He hoped this fight had nothing to do with his mother. All these years he'd believed that no one knew about the affair between his father and Daisy Dennison. Was he only kidding himself?

Charity glanced into the rearview mirror. "You realize you're blocking traffic?"

He started to tell her he didn't have time for food or gossip, but if Nina's body was in her car in a ravine, then leaving Charity alone in town was too dangerous, given everything that had happened lately.

Mitch was only one of a half dozen sheriffs who covered remote areas of Oregon alone. When he needed help, he could call the state for backup—or deputize locally. Most of the time, though, he handled things just fine on his own. Having Charity where he could keep an eye on her would be the safest thing for her. As for him…well, that was another story.

He shifted into drive and got moving.

"Betty's is back that way," she said as he passed Florie's and left the city limits.

"I'm taking you into protective custody."

"Protective custody?" She seemed to like the sound of that. "Although unnecessary." She opened her purse and pulled out the small gun he'd seen the night before, a can of pepper spray and a set of handcuffs.

He groaned. "What the hell do you plan to do with the cuffs?"

"I might have to detain someone until you can get there to save me." She grinned. "Unless you can think of something else to do with them."

"Don't make me sorry I didn't just lock you up at the jail."

"Where are we going?"

"To check on an anonymous call about a red compact in a ravine."

She looked over at him in surprise. "Nina?"

"Maybe."

She shivered and looked out at the highway ahead. "We still don't know who she is, right?"

"No." He drove out of town to the hypnotic sounds of the falling rain, the hum of the heater and the rhythmic sweep of the wipers, trying to ignore Charity's warm tantalizing scent.

Charity took off her rain jacket and tossed it in the back, making him too aware of the way her rust-colored turtleneck sweater brought out the gold in her eyes, not to mention how it hugged her full breasts.

He cracked his window open to let in a little of the cool damp air. Charity smiled as if she not only knew exactly what she did to him, but also enjoyed every minute of it.

Fog hung in the trees on both sides of the road like cotton ticking. A thin white mist swirled restlessly on the blacktop ahead of them. Not far out of town, they lost all traffic. This part of the state was isolated. Nothing but a narrow stretch of secondary two-lane highway hemmed in by dense coastal growth. The closest town, Oakridge, was a twenty-mile drive.

Unfortunately there were only a couple more hours of daylight left. Between that and the rain, the day was dark and gloomy enough without going looking for a dead body.

"So tell me about this alleged fight between Wade and Daisy," he said to keep his mind off what was up the road.

He didn't really mind having company on the drive to break the monotony. And as long as he kept pretending he wasn't susceptible to Charity's charms, he'd be fine.

"Wade and Daisy fought all the time, but this night it was huge."

"According to…?"

"You know I can't reveal my sources."

"Of course not."

"The nanny, Alma Bromdale, told my source in strictest confidence that she put Angela to bed, then went down to get the cold medicine she'd left in the kitchen."

The cold pills that had knocked Alma out and the reason she hadn't heard someone break into the house and take the baby, he thought remembering Alma's statement.

"Daisy was in the den just down the hall from the kitchen with Wade. Alma heard Wade tell Daisy that if Angela turned out not to be his, he'd throw her and the baby out without a cent, put her back on the street where he'd found her, and she'd never see Desiree again."

"What?"

"It's true. My source found out that Daisy's family was dirt poor. It was all an act, her being from money. She only married Wade for his."

That was no surprise, Mitch thought. But if Daisy was poor and Angela was another man's baby… All he could think about was what Daisy had told him earlier. That she'd loved his father. "If Wade wasn't the father, who was?" he asked, his stomach tightening. Was it possible Angela had been his half sister?

Charity shook her head. "I haven't been able to find out."

Knowing Charity, it wouldn't be long. "How was Alma able to hear all this? Wouldn't Wade and Daisy try to keep this sort of thing to themselves?"

"When it got really heated, Wade closed the den door, but Alma opened the dumbwaiter and could hear just fine."

He shook his head, wondering how any secrets were ever kept in this world. "If any of this is true, then why did it take so long to come out?"

"Daisy supposedly fired Alma. However, right after that, Alma came into a bunch of money and disappeared. My source stayed in touch with her through a friend. The only reason my source is talking now is that Alma is dead. Died of cancer the middle of September in Washington."

Damn, he'd hoped to talk to Alma about the baby spoon. "So there's no way to prove any of this?"

Charity smiled. "Alma has a sister, Harriet Bromdale, and she still lives in Coos Bay."

The only Bromdale in the Coos Bay phone book was Alma's sister? And leave it to Charity to come up with that nugget of information.

"I think Daisy paid Alma to keep quiet," Charity said.

"About some fight they had?"

She shook her head. "About the kidnapping."

He laughed. "Let me guess? You have a theory."

"Daisy couldn't let Wade find out that Angela wasn't his. She'd lose Desiree, and she and Angela would be out on the street. So Daisy hired someone to steal Angela. That's why Daisy's been a recluse all these years. She had to give up one child to save the other and has had trouble living with the bargain she made with the devil.'' Charity said all this as if she knew it for a fact. "Why else has Daisy locked herself up in that house?''

He glanced over at her. Sometimes her imagination amazed him. "It's as good a theory as any I've come up with.''

She smiled that killer smile of hers.

"But if Nina is Angela, what does that do to your theory? Wouldn't Daisy be delighted to see her daughter after all these years?''

Charity shook her head. "Not if it would expose her affair. Also not if her daughter was blackmailing her.''

He felt a sliver of ice run the length of his spine as he stared at Charity. It was one hell of a theory. What bothered him most was that it made a morbid kind of sense.

"Of course, I have a counter-theory,'' Charity said. "Wade got rid of the baby. Daisy knows it but can't prove it. So now she's living in seclusion with a monster she created. If she hadn't flaunted her affair, Angela would be alive. So she holds herself responsible for what happened to Angela. But at least she has Desiree—and she's still Mrs. Wade Dennison—and still living in the big house with all his money.''

He smiled over at her. "A counter-theory, huh? Either way makes Daisy sound pretty callous. What if Angela was Wade's?"

"Even better," Charity said. "He got rid of his own child. Imagine how that must weigh on her. The irony. And she has only herself to blame."

"Oh, I think Daisy would see Wade behind bars if she really believed he'd abducted her baby," Mitch said, but both of Charity's theories were as plausible as any he'd come up with.

The Lost Creek Falls sign suddenly appeared in the patrol car's headlights and he slowed, sorry he hadn't locked Charity up in jail, rather than bring her along. He hadn't seen another car in miles and he didn't like the bad feeling he was getting.

As he turned off onto the paved road to the falls, the fog grew thicker. The paved road ended a few miles later in a small parking lot at the top of the falls.

Mitch stopped at the end of the paved road, rolled down his window and looked out.

There were two sets of tracks in the muddy road past the falls. A motorcycle had gone in and come back out. And a truck by the look of the tread. If Nina's car was down here, then it had been driven in before the rains began.

As he looked down the road into the darkness of the rain and forest, he could see his breath in the chilly air. His brother, Jesse, wasn't the only one who owned a motorcycle, he told himself.

He rolled up his window, suddenly sick with worry as he started up the muddy narrow logging road.

"What a great place to dispose of a car," Charity whispered as limbs scraped the top of the patrol car and the tires kicked mud up under the wheel wells. "Or a body."

"Perfect place for an ambush, too," Mitch said.

Charity shot him a look, then locked her side of the car, making him smile. Sometimes the woman showed enough sense to endear her to him.

The headlights cut a swatch through the darkness. The only sound was the *whap, whap* of the wipers and the rain pounding the roof.

Half a mile in, the headlights picked up something through the rain. The shine of a chrome bumper. He felt Charity tense beside him as he slowed.

The red car had gone down a steep slope, ending up at the bottom of the ravine, partially hidden under the limbs of a large pine.

Mitch slowed to a stop, put on the emergency brake and pulled his binoculars from the glove compartment. He opened his door and stepped out into the rain and growing darkness. The car had torn through the thick vegetation along the slope to come to a crashing halt against the large pine.

He wiped moisture from the binocular lens and looked again, trying to decide if he should go down there now, with so little daylight left. He didn't like the idea of leaving Charity alone, and he knew that the compact had been driven in here days ago, before the rain. That meant Tuesday, the night Nina had disappeared, or early the next morning before the rain began. Could Nina still be alive if she'd survived the crash?

He didn't know. But it was the reason he couldn't put off going down there until morning.

THROUGH THE RAIN, Charity could see the rear of the red car where it had come to rest under the tree. Hugging herself, she looked over at Mitch as he got back into the car. "You're going to think I'm as deluded as Florie, but I'm picking up really bad vibes here."

He smiled reassuringly at her, his gaze meeting hers. "I won't be long."

"And if I never see you again?"

"The patrol car is four-wheel drive. If you go slowly, you'll be able to get out of here—if I don't come back."

"You're scaring me."

"I'm just covering all the bases." He climbed out again and went around to the back of the patrol car.

Against her better judgment, she climbed out, too, and watched as he pulled on a pair of overalls he'd taken from the back, along with a pair hiking boots.

"Shouldn't you call for backup?" she asked. It was getting dark and she couldn't shake the feeling that someone was watching them.

"We'd have to drive out to the highway to get the radio to work. And it would take several hours for the state police to get here. We only have about an hour left of daylight as it is. I'm not even sure it's

Nina's car or I would have you drive out and call for backup.''

She hated it when he was so logical. She glanced tentatively over the side of the steep ravine. It made her dizzy and sick to think he was actually about to go down there.

"Don't worry, I'll walk around to where it isn't so steep. It could take me a while, though. I want you to stay in the car and lock the doors. Give me until half an hour past dark. If I'm not back by then, drive out until the radio works and call for help.''

He swung a backpack over one shoulder and looked at her as if he was afraid to leave her alone. That made two of them.

"I have my gun and pepper spray,'' she said.

"Oh, yeah.'' He made it sound like she had a poisonous snake in her purse. ''And handcuffs. Don't forget those.''

"You aren't making fun of me, are you?''

"You know me better than that.''

"You should be glad I'm armed and can protect myself.''

He didn't seem to take comfort in that. ''We'll discuss the legality of carrying a concealed weapon without a permit when I get back.''

"It will give us something to talk about on the ride back to town,'' she said sarcastically.

He pointed to the patrol car, apparently waiting for her to get in it before he left.

She marched to the driver's side, opened the door and slid in, then locked the doors. As he started past to head up the road, he hesitated as if he might stop and say something more to her. It was one of those times that ''I have always loved you'' would have been appropriate.

Instead, he continued up the road, his back to her.

Impulsively she rolled down her window and yelled after him, ''In case you never come back—'' he slowed, his back still to her ''—I'll miss you!''

He continued walking as if he hadn't heard her. But she knew he had. Why hadn't she said that she loved him?

Because that wasn't what he wanted to hear, she told herself as she rolled up her window and settled in for a long wait. She put the loaded Derringer on the seat beside her, the pepper spray within reach. The keys were in the ignition.

It began to rain harder. The windows fogged up instantly. She thought about starting the car, letting the heater run, clearing the windows, but feared using up the gas. She might need it more later.

It made her nervous, not being able to see what was just outside the car. She wiped at the fogged-over glass, and the surface instantly skimmed over again with condensation. When she looked at her watch, she realized Mitch had only been gone five minutes.

MITCH WALKED down the road until he found a game trail that dropped down the steep wet slope. He cautiously descended, then worked his way through the wet slick vegetation.

It was getting dark fast and the rain wasn't letting up. Thick fog began to fill the ravine. He tried to move faster, thinking of Charity up on the road waiting for him, worried what she might do. He hadn't wanted to leave her alone, but then, he should never have brought her. Maybe she would have been safer back in town. With Charity, it really was a toss-up.

Ahead, he thought he caught a glimpse of chrome. He pulled the flashlight from his backpack and shone it into the dense foliage. It flickered off a piece of chrome trim.

He worked his way closer, his breath coming out in white puffs. The fog was growing denser, the slit of sky overhead darker.

A chill crept up his spine as he shone the flashlight through the branches and saw the red compact.

The car had come to rest at an odd angle at the base of a pine tree among the rocks. The front end was tilted down, the rear barely visible beneath the limbs of the pine tree.

He wondered again how the anonymous caller had found the car, fearing the only person who knew where Nina's vehicle was the one responsible for its being there. He recalled the motorcycle tracks in the muddy road.

As he neared the rear of the car, he could see that the trunk was open—and empty. The branches of the tree completely blocked the driver's side of the car. He worked his way a little more deeply into the ravine and climbed under the pine boughs on the passenger side. By standing on a rock, he was the same height as the passenger-side window.

He shone the light into the car, bracing himself.

The driver's seat was empty.

But there was something on the floor. He pulled himself up to get a closer look. In the beam of his flashlight he saw a Dennison duck decoy. The duck had been only partially painted; the rest appeared to be covered in dried blood and bits of human tissue.

He shone his flashlight into the back seat, already knowing what he'd find. Nina Monroe's bludgeoned body.

Chapter Thirteen

Friday, October 30

It was morning by the time the state police were able to get Nina's body into the coroner's van and secure the area. The forensics team arrived at first light to go over Nina's car.

From the car's registration in the glove compartment, the body was identified as Nina Bromdale. The same last name as the woman who'd been Angela Dennison's nanny twenty-seven years ago.

Mitch could feel the pieces coming together. According to Charity, Alma Bromdale had died in mid-September. Right after that, Nina had showed up in Timber Falls and gotten a job painting decoys at Dennison Ducks.

He glanced over at Charity as they passed Lost Creek Falls. She looked tired and pale, the night's events taking a toll on her, but incredibly beautiful. He knew she must be starving. He'd offered to drive her home but she'd wanted to stay with him—and he hadn't wanted to leave the crime scene unprotected.

"I'll buy you breakfast in Oakridge," he said.

She shot him a look. "We're going to Coos Bay to talk to Alma Bromdale's sister."

He'd seen the wheels turning in her head from the moment he'd told her Nina's real last name.

As they neared the highway, he saw a car pull up next to the deputy's vehicle blocking the road. Wade Dennison got out of the car and approached the deputy.

Wade looked up as Mitch stopped the patrol car and got out. "Stay here, okay?" he said to Charity.

She was looking at Wade. Mitch saw her shiver. "No problem."

"What the hell is going on?" Wade yelled through the rain the moment he saw Mitch coming toward him. "This damned deputy won't tell me a thing."

"Let's talk in your car," Mitch said as he walked to Wade's Lincoln and got in. The engine was running, the inside of the vehicle warm and spacious.

Wade climbed behind the wheel, breathing hard from the fury he had going. And maybe from fear, Mitch thought.

"We found Nina's car," he said.

Wade's head jerked around. It was clear he'd feared that was the case.

"Nina was inside. She's dead, Wade." He wasn't sure what reaction he'd been expecting. Certainly not the one he got.

"No." It came out a wail. Wade fell over the steering wheel, his head on his arms, his body racked with sobs.

Mitch waited until Wade got himself under control again. "Nina wasn't just your employee."

Wade wiped his eyes. "I can't talk about this now." His voice sounded hoarse, raspy.

"Wade—"

"Get out of my car. Please, Mitch. I can't just now, all right?" Wade had never called him by his first name. It was always Tanner. Or Sheriff. And Wade sure as hell had never said please.

Mitch could see that he wasn't going to get anywhere with Wade right now. He got out, then watched as Wade took off, driving too fast. Headed for Timber Falls.

Mitch turned and walked back to the patrol car and Charity.

"What kind of reaction was that?" she asked, no longer looking tired or scared as the reporter in her came out.

"Odd."

"Did he tell you what was up with him and Nina?"

Mitch shook his head. He didn't even want to admit to himself just how scared he was that Nina's death had started a chain reaction of events that would change Timber Falls forever.

He looked over at Charity, studying her as if he'd never seen her clearly before. The rain had stopped. Droplets glistened in the sunlight all around them. The flecks in Charity's eyes shone golden, her hair a wild flame of color.

She wasn't just beautiful. There was something so

alive about her. So filled with energy and excitement and life. He realized he was glad right now that she was so...Charity.

"What?" she asked.

He shook his head and smiled. "I was just wondering if we're going to be able to get pie in Oakridge."

HARRIET BROMDALE lived in an old farmhouse just outside Coos Bay. The house had once been white just like the picket fence, but the sea air had turned it gray over the years. Several pots of petunias still bloomed on the sidewalk beside the door as Charity waited beside Mitch for someone to answer his knock.

He'd been acting strangely all morning and she still couldn't believe he'd let her tag along. He hadn't even said the words "off the record" once.

An elderly woman wearing a striped waitress's uniform and worn white shoes answered the door. Her hair was pulled back from a face wrinkled and lined. She looked too old even to be Alma's older sister.

"Whatever you're selling, I'm not buying." She started to close the door.

"I'm Sheriff Mitch Tanner from Timber Falls," Mitch said, flashing his badge.

"Timber Falls?" Harriet shook her head. "What's she done now?"

"I beg your pardon?"

"Nina." She squinted at them. "That is why you're here, isn't it?"

"Then you do know Nina," he said.

"Know her?" The woman let out a harsh laugh. "I raised her. Not that she listened to anything I ever had to say."

"So you're her…"

"Aunt." She squinted at him. "Isn't that what you wanted to talk to me about?"

"Yes. I also wanted to ask about your sister, Alma."

Harriet pursed her lips. "Like mother, like daughter."

Charity felt Mitch's gaze on her. "Nina was Alma's daughter?" Charity asked.

The older woman looked at her, then Mitch. "Isn't that what I just said?"

"Would you mind if we came in for a few minutes?" Mitch asked.

Harriet hesitated, eyes small and hooded like a snake's as she looked at him. "I have to get to work soon."

"We won't take up any more of your time than we have to," he said, and she stepped back to let them in.

The house was dark inside and had that old closed-up smell, heightened by the odor of stale cigarette smoke. Harriet led them into a living room, motioning to a broken-down couch covered in what looked like the original plastic from when it was purchased probably fifty years ago.

Harriet sat in a threadbare recliner across from them, shook a cigarette from the pack in her uniform pocket and touched the flame of a lighter to the end. She took a deep drag, exhaled and squinted at the two of them through the smoke. "So what's Nina done now?"

Mitch had taken off his hat and now held it in his hands. "I'm sorry to have to tell you that she's dead. Apparent homicide."

The older woman let out a snort. "I'm not surprised. The boyfriend do it?"

"What boyfriend would that be?"

Harriet shrugged. "Some no-count. She sure could pick 'em. They never lasted long enough for me to get their names."

"When was the last time you saw Nina?"

"A month ago. I told her not to go to Timber Falls. Look what happened to her mother up there."

Charity figured Harriet was referring to Angela Dennison's abduction—and Alma's subsequent firing, but Harriet added, "Ended up pregnant."

"Alma was pregnant when she returned from Timber Falls?"

"Dropped off a baby for me to raise," Harriet said.

"You're sure it was her baby?" Charity had to ask, thinking of Angela. She could feel Mitch's gaze and belatedly remembered her promise just to sit quietly and let him do the talking.

The old woman frowned. "Of course it was her baby."

"You said you raised Nina? Do you have her birth certificate?" Mitch asked.

"I got a copy. You're wondering who the father is, right? Well, it wasn't on the birth certificate, and Alma would never tell. He was married. Why else would he give her all that money unless it was to keep her mouth shut?"

Charity shot Mitch an I-told-you-so look.

"Alma ran off right after dropping that bawling baby off, leaving me to raise the brat," Harriet was saying. "You think it's easy raising a kid by yourself? Did Nina appreciate the sacrifices I made? Ha. She always thought she deserved better."

"Could I see that copy of her birth certificate?" Mitch asked.

Harriet glanced at her watch, made an unpleasant face and pushed herself out of the recliner, then left the room. Charity could hear her rummaging around in a nearby room. The old woman returned after a few minutes and handed Mitch an Oregon birth certificate for Nina Ann Bromdale. Charity leaned close enough to read it. Nina was born in March—just two months after Angela Dennison, then three months old, had been taken from her crib in Timber Falls.

"How old was the baby when Alma left her with you?" Charity just had to ask.

Harriet shrugged. "Six, eight months old." It was obvious it made no difference to her.

"Do you mind if I take this?" Mitch asked, holding up the certificate.

"Keep it. I don't want it," Harriet said. "I imagine

you'll want me to bury her. Just got through burying her mother in September. Cancer.'' The woman nodded as if Alma had brought the cancer on herself.

"Alma say anything about Nina's father before she died?'' Mitch asked.

Harriett glared down at the cigarette between her fingers. "I didn't even hear she was dead until Nina came back from Mexico and told me. On her deathbed she had someone track down Nina, just had to tell Nina a bunch of stuff that she knew would set the girl off.''

"Like what?'' Charity asked.

"Maybe about the girl's father. Alma wasn't even cold in her grave before Nina took off for Timber Falls, saying she was going to finally get what she deserved. Guess she did.''

"I don't think anyone deserves to be murdered,'' Mitch said.

Harriet barked a laugh. "You didn't know Nina now, did you.''

"So Nina went to Timber Falls to see her father?''

"See him?'' Harriet let out another sarcastic bark. "She hated him. Blamed him for everything. She went up there to blackmail every last cent out of him, then make him pay. That's what she said, 'make him damned sorry.'''

"Did Alma ever talk about the baby that was abducted while she was a nanny in Timber Falls?'' Mitch asked.

Harriet took a puff on her cigarette. "Those rich people's baby? They fired Alma over it.''

"What was her side of the story?" Mitch asked.

"She said she didn't know nothin'." Harriet rolled her eyes. "I wouldn't be surprised if Alma had something to do with that baby disappearing."

"Why do you say that?" Mitch asked.

"All that money she supposedly got from her baby's father," Harriet said. "What man would do that?"

Charity looked at Mitch.

"Didn't you ever wonder if maybe the baby your sister brought you was the Dennison's missing baby?" he asked.

"I'm no fool," Harriet said, sounding angry. "But I also know when to keep my mouth shut. Didn't have nothin' to do with me."

Charity watched Mitch rake his hand through his hair in frustration. "Have you ever seen this?" Mitch said as he pulled the baby spoon out of his pocket.

Harriett started to reach for it, but then pulled her hand back. "That belonged to that baby, didn't it?"

He nodded. "Did Alma ever show it to you?"

She shook her head violently.

"Nina had this spoon," he said.

Harriett got to her feet a little unsteadily. "I have to get to work."

Mitch and Charity got to their feet, as well. "If you think of anything else…" Mitch handed Harriet his card.

She took it reluctantly, as if she thought it might contaminate her. "It's that town. It's evil."

MITCH COULD TELL that Charity was bursting at the seams to say something. "Nina Ann Bromdale could have been Angela," she said the moment they were in the patrol car. "Even if the birth certificate is real, Harriet had no idea how old Nina was when she got her."

He nodded. "But nothing is definite without DNA testing, and I'm not sure Wade will agree to it."

"That's crazy. If Nina was Angela... You don't think Wade would kill his own daughter?"

Mitch shook his head, remembering Wade's reaction. "I think there's more to the story and I'm not convinced Nina *was* Angela."

Charity was quiet for a few miles. "The town isn't evil."

"It's the rain," he said. "The rain and the isolation, the dark days trapped inside. It makes people in Timber Falls crazy."

She looked over at him. "So why do you stay?"

The question took him by surprise. He frowned, unable to answer.

Charity was smiling smugly as if she thought she knew the reason. He'd only left long enough to graduate from college. She'd left only long enough to get her journalism degree. Did she think he only stayed because she was there?

"I want to talk to the jeweler in Eugene who made the baby spoon," he said, changing the subject. "But I would imagine you're hungry again, aren't you?"

They ate in a small café overlooking the water. Charity had fried oysters, French fries and coleslaw, followed by a piece of coconut-cream pie. He had the red snapper, but he hardly tasted it. He couldn't quit thinking about Nina and Wade and Angela, and those damned motorcycle tracks in the mud. Or what Harriet had said about Nina coming back from Mexico to see her mother. Mexico.

"This pie isn't as good as Betty's," Charity said, and smiled at him.

Why did he stay in Timber Falls? He had a bad feeling it was because of the woman across the table from him. And an even worse feeling that she knew it.

A NICELY DRESSED gray-haired woman looked up from behind the counter at Hart's Jewelry as they entered.

The woman's face brightened at the sight of them. "Good afternoon. Let me guess. You're looking for an engagement ring. I can always tell."

Mitch saw Charity's face redden with embarrassment. His own stomach tightened. "We're here on official business," he said, and flashed his badge.

"I'm sorry, I just... What can I help you with, Sheriff? I'm Lois Hart, the owner."

Charity wandered over to a display case. He watched her admire a silver bracelet as he took the baby spoon from his pocket and set it gingerly on the glass counter.

The clerk picked it up, seeming to recognize it.

"I understand this spoon was made here, designed

especially for Wade Dennison of Dennison Ducks,'' Mitch said, watching her face.

''My husband made it.'' Her voice broke and Mitch knew what was coming: ''He died four years ago.''

''I'm sorry. How many of these did your husband make?''

''Two sets. One for the first baby, engraved with that baby's name, and a second for the new baby. Mr. Dennison was very explicit. He made my husband promise never to make another set like them. Of course my husband never did.''

''You're sure this is your husband's work?''

''Oh, yes,'' she said with a soft smile.

''No one ever requested he make another set?''

She shook her head. ''We were just sick when we heard about what happened, someone stealing that baby. Was she ever found?''

He shook his head.

She held out the baby spoon to him as if she no longer liked holding it. ''What kind of monster would do that?''

Mitch wished he knew. ''Well, thank you for your time,'' he said as he took the spoon and pocketed it again. Charity was still at the display counter looking at the silver bracelet again. ''Here is my card if you think of anything else.''

''Sorry about that mix-up back there,'' he said as he and Charity headed for his patrol car.

She gave him a small smile. ''I've pretty much accepted that I'm going to be an old maid.''

He laughed. "I can't see you as an old maid." He hated the thought of Charity not being loved and cherished and cared for. She deserved more. But he also hated the thought of her with another man. "But then, you already have the cat."

She made a face. "Where to now?"

He pulled his keys out of his pocket as they reached the patrol car. "I just remembered something I forgot to ask Mrs. Hart. Wait for me in the car for a minute?"

She nodded and took the keys.

He trotted back to the store. Lois Hart looked up in surprise. "There's a silver bracelet my friend was looking at." He pointed to the one Charity hadn't been able to take her eyes off. "Would you wrap it? I'd like to buy it."

Lois Hart smiled. "So I *was* right about the two of you."

Mitch didn't bother to correct her. As he walked back to the patrol car and Charity, he felt the small wrapped jewelry box in his pocket and wondered what had possessed him. He couldn't give it to her. She'd get the wrong impression, and that would only make things worse between them.

He cursed his moment of weakness. He hadn't thought. He'd just wanted her to have the bracelet.

"Did you ask her the question you forgot?" Charity inquired as he climbed behind the wheel.

"Yeah." He turned on the ignition, the small package in his pocket feeling as weighty as the silver spoon.

On the way back to Timber Falls, Charity gave up trying to draw him into conversation and finally curled up and slept.

Mitch got the call just outside of town. "Nina Bromdale's got a sheet on her," the trooper from the state police informed him. He rattled off a series of arrests for shoplifting, misdemeanor theft and driving while under the influence. "Her last arrest was in San Diego. She and her boyfriend were both picked up after a city cop pulled her over. The boyfriend was driving. He got a DUI. She got thirty days for resisting arrest and disorderly conduct."

"Boyfriend?"

"Let me check here. Yeah. Name's Jesse Tanner. Tanner. Any relation?"

"Afraid so." Jesse hadn't just known Nina, he'd shared the back seat of a cop car with her. Mitch felt sick. So much for his brother's coming back to Timber Falls because he was homesick—or to steal Charity. Jesse had come back because of Nina. But what worried Mitch were the motorcycle tracks on the road into where Nina's car—and body—were found.

Charity was snuggled against the passenger-side door sound asleep when he pulled up in front of his house. When he went around and opened the passenger-side door, she practically tumbled into his arms, stirring just long enough to wrap her arms around his neck.

As he carried her into the house, she sighed against his neck and smiled in her sleep, murmuring something that sounded…like banana cream?

By the time he lowered her to the bed in the spare room, she was snoring softly. He smiled to himself as he slipped off her boots and drew the quilt over her. Then he stood for a moment just looking down at her.

How was he going to protect her from herself?

That was when he remembered her cat. He called her house. Florie had gone home it seemed. He dug a can of tuna out of his kitchen cabinet and walked next door with Charity's house key from her purse.

"Winky? Winky?" In the kitchen he opened the tuna. Still no cat. Didn't most cats come running when they heard the can opener? Leave it to Charity to have a cat that was the exception to the rule.

He put the can of tuna on the floor and glanced around. No cat. Why was he surprised she even had a cat? He locked up behind him and hurried back to his house.

Charity was still fast asleep. He shook his head, smiling to himself, then stretched out, fully clothed, on the couch in the next room. She was safe. At least for tonight. He closed his eyes, listening to the sound of her breathing on the other side of the wall, no longer kidding himself.

He stayed in Timber Falls because of Charity.

Chapter Fourteen

Halloween

Charity opened her eyes, the remnants of the dream still clinging and the blinding daylight coming through the window. She didn't want to leave the dream—and Mitch, who was wearing that black tuxedo again and looked so handsome....

She blinked. Why were the curtains open? Why were there no curtains at all? She blinked again. Because it wasn't her bedroom. It wasn't her bed. It wasn't even her house!

She sat up with a start, not sure for a moment where she was. Then she saw Mitch's uniform hat on a bureau by the door and through the open doorway, spotted his boots off the end of the couch.

She pulled down the quilt, disappointed to see that she was fully dressed. Darn. Slipping her legs over the side of the bed, she got up and tiptoed into the living room, trying to piece together last night.

Something told her nothing had happened between her and Mitch. Nothing at all. The man either had the strength of will of a saint or she wasn't as irresistible as she'd hoped. That was an awful thought.

Then she reminded herself she was holding out for marriage. Right.

Mitch was sound asleep on the couch. He looked wonderful. She leaned closer to study his handsome face. Suddenly he grabbed her, flipped her over on the couch and was on top of her before she knew what was happening.

"NEVER SNEAK UP on a man of the law," he growled down at her. "I could have shot you."

She smiled. "You would never shoot me. You might want to but—"

He silenced her with a kiss, drawing her into his arms without even thinking. She was still warm from sleep, soft in all the right places, her mouth so absolutely perfect. He could have kissed her until Christmas—

He jerked back at the sound of someone banging on his front door. Past Charity, he could see Wade Dennison's large frame through the bamboo blinds. Damn. Mitch looked at Charity. Desire burned bright in her eyes, making him weak in the knees. This woman would be the death of him. But the pounding on the door was too insistent to ignore.

"I need to talk to Wade," he said as rolled off her. Wade had saved him. So why wasn't he happy about that?

"I need to go to the paper," Charity said. "You

aren't going to try to stop me from doing the story on Nina's murder, are you?''

He heard the challenge in her voice. "I'm no fool." That, of course, was debatable. He couldn't keep her from doing the story any more than he could keep her with him 24/7, and they both knew it.

"But you're taking a deputy with you," he said. "No arguments." He picked up his cell phone and made the call as he tried to calm down physically before opening the door.

She didn't argue as she sashayed into the spare bedroom for her shoes. Mitch went to the front door and opened it.

"I have to talk to you." Wade shot a look at Charity as she swept past him, but had the good sense not to say anything. The moment the door closed behind Charity, Wade crossed to a chair and slumped into it.

"Nina was my daughter," Wade said, and put his head in his hands.

Mitch sat down. "Angela?"

"Angela?" Wade raised his head and frowned. "Not Angela. Nina. Aren't you listening to me? Do I have to spell it out for you? I had an affair with Alma."

Mitch stared at him. "Alma? Alma was pregnant with your baby?"

He nodded. "Daisy was pregnant and driving me crazy. There were rumors that the baby wasn't mine..." He waved a hand. "Alma overheard us arguing one night and…comforted me after Daisy went to bed….'' He stopped and looked up.

''Alma got pregnant?''

Wade nodded.

''How much money did you give her to keep quiet?''

''Quiet?'' Wade shook his head, his brow furrowing. ''No, I gave her money to take care of our baby.''

Mitch decided not to argue the point. ''Wade, I know Nina came to Timber Falls to blackmail you.''

''It wasn't like that. She was my daughter. Of course I'd give her money. I just wanted to help her.''

''How much *help* was Nina demanding?''

Wade shot up out of the chair. ''This is exactly why I didn't tell you,'' he said angrily. ''I knew you'd try to make more out of this than it was. Nina wanted to do something with her life. I offered to help. I gave her a job. I offered her money.''

Mitch took a deep breath. ''Wade, if she was your daughter, then why keep it a secret?''

The older man closed his eyes and wagged his large head as he sank back down again. ''I couldn't do that to Daisy. You know how she's been since Angela disappeared. I couldn't spring this daughter on her. Daisy and I spent years trying to find Angela, following up every lead only to reach another dead end. Nina understood that I couldn't tell Daisy. In fact, she insisted we keep it between the two of us. She didn't want to destroy my life. She just needed a little help to realize her dreams.''

The Nina everyone described wouldn't have let Wade off that easily. "What was the price of those dreams?"

Wade's gaze narrowed, and anger sparked again in his eyes. "You're one cynical bastard, aren't you, Tanner."

Mitch waited.

"A million." He held up a hand. "It was money I'd put away for Angela twenty-seven years ago. I got lucky in a couple of investments." He shrugged.

He had given Nina Angela's money? Mitch wondered how Daisy would have taken that if she'd found out. "A million dollars is a lot of dreams. What if Angela turned up?" Or was Wade sure she never would?

"Nina was my daughter," Wade said defensively.

"You know that for sure?" Mitch had to ask.

"Alma was a virgin the night... I know, okay?" He shook his head. "Don't you believe anything anyone tells you?"

"Not really. So when were you going to give her the money?"

"I'd already put it in an account for her. I was to meet her at the plant Tuesday night to give her all the paperwork, but she wasn't there. Then when I didn't hear from her or she didn't show up at the plant...."

"What time were you to meet her?"

"Ten. I got there, but there was no sign of her."

Mitch rubbed his forehead. "Why were you so sure she'd come to harm?"

Wade sighed. "She wouldn't have walked away from the money, all right?" He sounded tired, defeated, a broken man.

Mitch could only imagine how Nina had worn him down until he promised to give her a million dollars. "Did you hire a private investigator to follow Charity?"

Wade frowned. "Why would I do that?"

"Just a day ago you threatened to kill her."

"I was angry and upset. But I certainly didn't hire anyone to follow her." He was still frowning, and Mitch wondered if he was worrying that Daisy might have hired the P.I.

"Did you ever employ a private investigator named Kyle L. Rogers out of Portland?" He could see that Wade had.

"If you're thinking that Daisy…"

"I'm just asking questions, Wade. That's what I do. I follow any lead I get and see where it goes." Mitch raked a hand through his hair. His head hurt. "Nina make any enemies that you know of?"

"She didn't get along with people all that well." No kidding. "She had trouble with the other painters, but I can't believe any of them—"

"Anyone else?"

Wade sighed. "I saw her arguing with Bud once, but everyone argues with Bud."

Mitch couldn't disagree with that. "Know what they argued about?"

Wade shrugged. "You'd have to ask Bud."

Bud had said they'd never spoken two words. "Where was this and when?"

"Outside the plant Monday afternoon."

So that's who Nina had been arguing with when Charity had seen her and taken her photo.

"Look, Wade, I know you were spying on Nina. Charity saw you in the trees. Why?"

"I was afraid she'd get in some sort of trouble before she left town."

"Or were you afraid she'd renege on your deal and tell everyone the truth?" What if there really was a letter from Nina to Charity? Maybe Wade just *feared* there was.

Wade got to his feet, his face turning bright red. "Maybe Nina would have been different if she'd had a father growing up."

Or maybe not. "I'm sorry about your daughter, but my job now is to find her killer. Did either Daisy or Desiree know about this financial arrangement you had with Nina?"

"Leave my family out of this."

"This is a murder investigation, Wade. Tell your family before I have to."

CHARITY WENT RIGHT to work on her stories, first writing about the Bigfoot sighting, which was starting to feel like old news, then the story about Nina Bromdale's murder.

She wished she had more information. But unfortunately Wade thwarted her attempts to talk to anyone who worked at Dennison Ducks. It seemed he'd told his staff that anyone who talked to the press would be fired.

She also couldn't print anything about the possibility of Nina being Angela Dennison. Not without proof. But how was she going to get proof?

As she sat down at her computer, she felt anxious—even with the Derringer, pepper spray and handcuffs in her purse and a deputy sitting in the corner. Nina had been murdered and the killer was still out there.

Worse, she knew Mitch wouldn't have put a deputy on her unless he thought she was in danger. That had to mean he bought her theory about the letter. He hardly ever bought her theories—and he'd kissed her three times in the past two days. That had to mean something, too, right?

She'd gone to her house, showered and changed before coming to the newspaper office, all the time knowing a deputy was not far away, but she still kept looking over her shoulder. As she went back over the past few days, she tried to imagine how all the pieces fit together. That was the problem. They didn't.

Worse, she didn't really have enough facts to do a story on the murder for this week. If only Nina really had written down her life story for Charity and—mailed it—and there really *was* a letter.

She looked up as the door opened. The deputy was already on his feet, hand on his revolver. "It's all right," she said, waving him back into his seat. "It's my assistant, Blaine."

Blaine didn't look any the worse for wear since

being bound and left in an alley. In fact, he looked downright cheerful as he came in. She noticed he had a sketchbook in his hand. "I drew you something."

She made room on her desk for the book.

"I heard you lost your photo of Nina Monroe. I saw her a few times when I took papers up to Dennison Ducks. So…" He flipped open the sketchbook.

Charity gasped as she stared down at a perfect likeness of Nina Bromdale, aka Monroe.

AFTER WADE LEFT, and with Charity gone, Mitch noticed how empty his house seemed. He stood in the middle of the room, his senses assaulted by her. He could still smell the light scent of her perfume. Still taste her on his lips.

He should have known that having Charity here even for one night was going to change the way he felt about a lot of things—including this house.

He couldn't imagine opening the door without feeling as if something was missing once her scent had faded and the cool quiet had settled back in.

As if he didn't have enough trouble, he noticed jack-o'-lanterns on porches and cardboard goblins taped in windows as he drove through town. Halloween. He'd almost forgotten. All he needed now was a full moon. Every weirdo in town would be going crazy tonight—and there was already a killer on the loose.

His first stop was the post office to check Charity's mailbox. More than ever he wondered if Charity wasn't right about Nina writing a letter to the paper.

But had the woman just been planning to expose her father? He couldn't forget the baby spoon he'd carried around in his jacket pocket.

Also from what he'd been told about Nina, he couldn't imagine that she'd just take the money and run. She'd wanted revenge. And a letter to the local paper gave credibility to Charity's attack at the post office.

But there was no letter from Nina in the newspaper post-office box. Charity would be disappointed that her theory wasn't panning out. No more disappointed than he was.

He wanted this case over and done with as quickly as possible. Letter or no letter Charity was in danger. He felt it, just a nagging feeling he couldn't shake.

He stopped by her office and gave her the mail from her post-office box, relieved to see she was busy at her computer with the deputy watching over her.

"No letter," Charity said seeing his face.

He shook his head. "If she'd mailed it before she was killed, it would have been here by now."

She nodded, then said, "Look what Blaine drew," she said excitedly.

He looked at the eerie likeness of Nina Bromdale on the computer screen next to the headline Quest to Find Father Ends in Murder. Under the sketch of Nina was the cutline "Who is this woman really?"

"Can we talk in the darkroom?" Mitch asked.

Charity smiled at him as if she thought it was just a ploy so he could kiss her again. She got to her feet and led the way to the darkroom. He closed the door behind them.

"I need to tell you something," he said.

"Let me guess. Off the record? See, I'm getting where I can read your mind."

He hoped not. "Wade was Nina's father."

"So she *was* Angela!"

"No. It seems he had an affair with Alma."

"Get out of here."

"All we have is Alma's word that the baby was even his. Until we run the DNA, I'm still skeptical," Mitch said. "But Wade believed it. He was planning to give Nina money the night she disappeared."

"How much?"

"A cool million."

Charity let out a whistle. "If Wade really is Nina's father, then he paid Alma to keep quiet about it and now Nina. Or at least claims he was going to pay her off before she was killed."

Mitch did love Charity's mind sometimes. She could have been a cop.

"You don't think Wade…"

"Killed her?" He shook his head. "I don't know. Nina sounds like she was pretty coldhearted. Wade had to know that when she went through that million she'd be back demanding more."

"You think there's more to the story, don't you," Charity said. "Angela's baby spoon."

He nodded. "I think maybe there was more blackmail involved than just her paternity. I think she might have known who kidnapped Angela."

Charity nodded. "That's exactly what I think."

Yeah. Mitch thought. Maybe the two of them were getting where they could read each other's mind. Now, that *was* a scary idea.

He stepped to the darkroom door. It was too tight in here, too intimate. "I have to go. If you need me, call."

She laughed softly. "I might take you up on that."

Outside again, he started the patrol car, her words echoing in his head. She'd always held out for marriage, and that had kept him safe. He didn't want to think of what would happen if Charity changed her mind.

He headed out of town, dreading what he had to do. He wasn't looking forward to confronting his brother Jesse. And the last thing he wanted to do was see his father. Maybe he'd luck out and the old man would be at the bar. *Huh,* he thought. *First time I've ever wished that.*

He hadn't seen his father in months and only then in passing. He couldn't remember the last time they'd spoken. When he'd left home at eighteen, it had been for good. He'd never been back.

Lee Tanner opened the door at Mitch's knock almost as if he'd been expecting him. Lee was a big man, handsome to a fault, and from old family money. The latter had proved to be a curse since it afforded his father too much time to drink. He wasn't a mean drunk. Mitch couldn't remember his father ever raising his voice. He was just a drunk.

"I need to see Jesse," Mitch said, looking past his

father. The house was neat as a pin. That surprised him. Nor did he pick up the smell of alcohol when his father said, "Jesse will be back shortly. Come on in, son."

The "son" grated, but Mitch didn't say anything. He hadn't come here to fight, just to try to get the truth out of Jesse. Who was he kidding? That would take a fight for sure, and even then Mitch couldn't trust that his brother would be truthful.

"It's good to see you," Lee said. "Can I offer you something to drink?"

"I don't drink."

Lee smiled. "I was thinking maybe a soda or a glass of iced tea. I have both."

Iced tea in this house? He'd believe it when he saw it. "Iced tea, then."

Lee walked into the kitchen, which was open to the living room, and took down two glasses before opening the fridge and pulling out a pitcher of iced tea. How about that? His father had definitely been expecting him. This had to be some kind of show.

Mitch glanced around the place, rather than watch his father fill the glasses. Lee had designed the house himself. At one time, he'd been an architect in Seattle. Then he'd married Ruth Marks, built this house and had two sons.

His father handed him a glass and took the other.

"Thanks." Mitch couldn't remember his father ever drinking iced tea.

"Have a seat. Jesse should be back soon."

"I'd rather stand."

His father took a sip of the tea and didn't even grimace at the taste. Maybe he'd put a little something in his.

"How long has Jesse been staying with you?" Mitch asked.

"Are you asking as a brother or a cop?"

"Does it matter?"

Lee smiled again. "Since late Saturday night. He'd called to say he was coming home and asked if he could stay here for a while." Lee looked up, meeting Mitch's gaze. "It sure is nice to have the company. I'm trying to talk him into staying longer."

"Is he thinking about leaving?" If Jesse left now, he'd only look all the more guilty.

"He wants a place of his own. He's considering buying the old Kramer land outside of town. I'm surprised, too. But I think he missed his home. I know he missed you. He's hoping to mend a few fences. He's changed, Mitch."

Mitch stared at his father, not believing a word of it. "Yeah, he says you've changed, too." He hadn't meant to sound so cynical.

Lee chuckled. "Hard to believe, huh."

"Next to impossible."

His father's smile never wavered. "Stranger things have happened."

"What would Jesse do in Timber Falls?"

"Didn't he tell you about his paintings? Your brother's quite the artist."

The back door slammed and Mitch heard the sound of approaching footsteps. Jesse used to draw some when they were kids, but since when had he become an artist? And since when had their father become so naive?

Lee Tanner turned toward Jesse as he came through the kitchen. "Mitch is here. Why don't the two of you go out on the deck for some privacy?" He downed the rest of his iced tea, then took the glass into the kitchen to rinse it out.

"Yeah, let's talk outside," Mitch said, putting his unfinished iced tea on the kitchen counter.

Jesse shrugged and opened the front door. They stepped out onto the covered deck that ran the length of the front of the house.

"So, little bro," Jesse said. "Glad to see you took my advice and came out."

"Tell me about Nina Bromdale."

Jesse walked to the railing and leaned against it. "I wondered how long it would take you."

"She was your girlfriend."

"*Was* is the key word here."

"She's why you came back to Timber Falls."

Jesse shook his head. "It's a lot more complicated than that. You ever meet her?"

Mitch shook his head.

"Lucky you."

"She's dead," Mitch said. "Murdered, but I think you already know that. I saw your bike tracks on the road where Nina's car was found."

Jesse didn't say anything. "You going to arrest me for her murder?"

Mitch hoped he'd never have to. "Did you kill her?"

"No, but what are the chances of you believing that?"

"Why don't you try telling me the truth?"

"I wasn't lying about missing you and Dad."

"And Charity?" Mitch had gotten a print off the stone heart.

Jesse's.

He smiled. "I admit I gave her the presents. Maybe I thought if she had a secret admirer, you might wake up and admit how you feel about her. Maybe I'd hoped she was available." He shrugged and grinned.

The latter sounded more like it. "It was you in her house the other night, wasn't it."

Jesse nodded. "I saw someone go around the back of her house. I scared him off, but the back window had been pried open."

Mitch had found that when he'd investigated the break-in, but that didn't mean Jesse hadn't been the one to do it. "So you just climbed in?"

"I wanted to make sure there wasn't anyone else in the house."

Mitch shook his head. "You always have an answer, don't you."

"Maybe it's just the truth," Jesse said.

"When was the last time you saw Nina?"

"Monday."

The day before she disappeared.

"I don't expect you to believe me, but I thought I could stop her."

"Stop her from what?"

Jesse rubbed his jaw. "Getting herself killed."

"You knew what she was doing here?"

"I knew Nina had this thing about finding her father and making him pay."

Making him pay. Just as Harriet had said. Just as Charity had theorized. "She tell you who her father was?"

Jesse shook his head. "She didn't know. Then she got this message from her mother. Next thing I heard she was in Timber Falls."

"You said you saw her Monday. Where?"

Jesse sighed. "At her bungalow. She told me to get lost."

"Come on, Jesse. You didn't just come up here to try to save Nina."

His brother smiled. "Okay, she ripped me off when she left. She took some things of mine." He saw Mitch's expression. "Some canvases, if must know. I'd been painting down in Mexico. Sold a few. She ripped me off when she left to go see her mother. I wanted the canvases back."

"Did you get them?"

"She'd already sold them. I was pissed. We argued. That was the last time I saw her." He paused. "You don't believe me."

"How did you know where her car was?"

Jesse sighed. "You told me that a black pickup

had been following Charity. I followed one out of town. It led me to the car.''

"You were the one who called it in?'' Mitch asked in surprise.

Jesse nodded.

"Why didn't you give Sissy your name?''

He shrugged. "Never did like talking to cops.''

"What about the truck?''

"I lost it. Or it lost me.''

Mitch took off his hat and raked a hand through his hair. "Any chance forensics is going to find your prints in that car?''

"I'd be surprised if they didn't. Nina and I spent the past four months together down south.''

"How *did* you hear that Nina was in Timber Falls?''

"Dad saw her and recognized her from a photo of the two of us in Mexico I'd sent him.''

Mitch stared at his brother for a moment, then turned to go. "Don't leave town.''

"Aren't you going to tell Dad goodbye?'' Jesse asked. "He's been on the wagon.''

"Right.''

"Cut him some slack, little bro. He's trying damned hard and all because of you.''

"Me?''

"That's right. He feels bad about the years he drowned himself in a bottle after our mother left.''

"He should. His running around is why she left us.''

"Like hell it is.''

Mitch started to leave again. "I don't want to hear this."

"Well, you're going to," Jesse said, grabbing his sleeve and jerking him around to face him. "All these years you've blamed Dad because she left us. It's time you heard the truth. She left because she never loved him or us. She married him because he had money and because the man she really loved had married someone else."

"That's a lie!" Mitch snapped, jerking free. "He was drinking and having an affair with Daisy Dennison."

Jesse shook his head. "I was older than you. I remember the night she told him she'd never loved him, never wanted us, would rather be dead than stay with him. He loved her, man, and he was devastated. She demanded money so she could leave. He refused to let her go."

"So he had an affair."

"I know you were only six, but don't you remember how she was with us?" Jesse asked. "All the mornings she stayed in bed, didn't even get up to see us off to school."

Her disinterest was because of their father's unfaithfulness. He could remember well their father standing at the stove frying bacon, the quiet in the house so loud it was deafening. "She was depressed because she was married to a cheating drunk."

"Dad finally gave her the money she needed to leave. I followed Dad into the woods that day." Jesse's throat moved as if the words were stones he could barely swallow. "He fell to the ground and... I've never seen anyone cry like that."

Mitch stared at his brother, the weight on his chest unbearable. He wanted to defend their mother, but nothing came out. His memories of the past that had once been so clear now felt so damaged that he couldn't make sense of them. His father putting an arm around his mother's shoulders. Her shrugging it off. The hurt in his father's eyes, the pain.

"She wasn't any good—"

"Don't," their father said from the doorway. "Your mother loved you both. She wanted to take you, but she wasn't strong enough to raise two boys on her own."

The lie hung in the air.

Mitch met Jesse's gaze, the truth like an arrow through his heart. He glanced at the doorway, but his father was gone.

Jesse stepped to Mitch and hugged him tightly. Tears in his eyes, he let go, turned and walked back toward the front door, leaving Mitch standing on the deck alone.

Mitch felt sick. Was it possible he'd been wrong about everything he'd believed? All these years, why hadn't his father said something? But he knew the answer to that. No one had wanted to admit just what kind of mother Mitch had really had.

His cell phone rang. "Yes?"

"Thought you'd want this right away," said the head of forensics. "We got two matches on that decoy we found in the victim's car. Her prints and an Ethel Whiting's."

Chapter Fifteen

It was late afternoon and the rain was making the day even darker when Ethel Whiting opened her front door.

"I wondered when you'd be back." She motioned Mitch into the parlor.

"Your fingerprints were found on the decoy that was used to kill Nina Bromdale," he said as followed her into her sitting room.

Ethel lowered herself into a chair. "Bromdale?"

"It seems she might be the nanny's daughter," Mitch said. "Alma and Wade's daughter."

Ethel's face seemed to crumble. "She wasn't Angela?"

"No." It was obvious she'd wanted to believe that Nina was Daisy's and some other man's besides Wade. "I think you should call your lawyer, Ethel."

She shook her head. "I would have told you yesterday, but I thought Nina was still alive when her body wasn't found at Dennison Ducks. I didn't go to the plant Tuesday night planning to kill her. At least I don't think so. I didn't know who she was, just that she posed a danger to Wade. I thought I could scare her into leaving him alone.'' She laughed softly. ''Nothing could scare that young woman. I could see that there wasn't enough money in the world to buy her off, either. We argued. She'd put down the duck she'd been painting. I hardly remember picking it up and hitting her.''

''Was she dead?''

She looked up. ''I thought so. I didn't check her pulse. I just dropped the decoy next to her body. I assumed as soon as you found her body and the murder weapon…''

''You knew your fingerprints were it?''

''Of course. And that they'd be on file. My parents had me fingerprinted as a child. They worried that because of their affluence, someone might kidnap me,'' Ethel said. ''Ironic, isn't it.''

''You didn't put Nina in her car and drive it into a ravine south of town?''

She gave him a sympathetic look. ''I am not a deceitful woman, Mitchell. I did nothing to cover my crime. I had some things I wanted to get in order and I preferred spending what days I had left here in the house. I've been waiting for you to arrest me.''

''What time did you go to the plant?'' he asked.

''A little before nine. Her car was in the lot. I knew she worked late a lot. Whatever that woman had on Wade, I could see what it was doing to him. I had to stop her.''

She'd done this for Wade. Mitch shook his head, remembering that Wade said he went to the plant at ten and Nina was gone. "Either Nina wasn't dead, or someone moved her body."

"Why would they do that?" Ethel asked.

"Is it possible Wade saw you leaving the plant Tuesday night? He found Nina's body and tried to cover for you?"

She shook her head. "Wade has made a lot of poor decisions in his life, but he would never cover up a murder."

Ethel had a lot more faith in Wade than Mitch did. But then, love was blind, wasn't it?

"I'll have someone come over to take you in."

She gave him a reproachful look. "I'll be right here, Mitchell."

As he was about to call headquarters, he got another call. This one from the state police. Private investigator Kyle L. Rogers's body had just been found in a motel room in Oakridge. He'd been shot at close range with a small-caliber weapon. His black pickup was nowhere to be found. "I'm on my way."

CHARITY HAD her latest edition out and on the streets by late afternoon. It was going to be her best-selling newspaper by all accounts. Blaine was out delivering papers. The deputy Mitch had guarding her was sitting in the corner, thumbing through a magazine.

She'd finished all her work and was thinking about Mitch when he walked through the door. She knew something was wrong the moment she saw him.

"Kyle Rogers's body had been found in a motel

in Oakridge. Homicide,'' Mitch told her and the deputy.

''I want you to go home, Charity. I've already called Florie. She's meeting you at the house.''

''Okay.'' He'd obviously expected her to argue and seemed surprised when she didn't. And pleased. Was it this easy to please the man?

''I have to run down to Oakridge, then I'll come by the house. I won't be long.''

''Don't worry about me,'' she told Mitch. ''I'm sure Florie will bring her baseball bat and I have an armed deputy. What more could a girl want?'' She wanted Mitch's strong arms around her. This being independent all the time was getting old.

''Promise me you'll put the gun and pepper spray away with all the kids out trick-or-treating tonight.''

She nodded. ''As soon as I get home.''

He glanced at the deputy. ''You'll stay with her?''

''Sure thing.''

Mitch walked her out to the deputy's car. The rain had stopped temporarily, but low-hunkering clouds cast an eerie glow over the town. Fog drifted out of the woods like ghosts to haunt the narrow streets.

Jack-o'-lanterns flickered in front of several businesses. With everything that had been happening, Charity realized she'd forgotten to buy treats for the kids. She'd have to stop on the way home.

''Be careful?'' Mitch said.

It was another one of those moments when a kiss would have been nice. But she couldn't see Mitch kissing her in front of the deputy. "I will," she said, then watched him drive away.

"We need to stop by the grocery store on the way home," she told the deputy once they were in his car. "I have to pick up some candy for the trick-or-treaters. My Aunt Florie will bring things like carob cookies or tofu popcorn balls. I really don't want to get my windows soaped and egged."

She thought he might argue with her. Or maybe she just expected all men to argue with her the way Mitch did. So she was a little perplexed when he just laughed.

Little ghosts and goblins were already out trick-or-treating. Halloween was a big deal in Timber Falls. Everyone got into the act at a huge costume party at the Duck-In. As the deputy drove her home from the grocery, they passed groups of children and adults dressed as vampires and zombies, aliens and witches.

Charity couldn't help but shiver. There was a killer out there, maybe closer than any of them thought.

A group of costumed kids skittered across the street in front of them, squealing and shrieking as the deputy pulled up in front of her house.

The kids clambered up the steps to the porch. A moment later Florie opened the door and began dispensing something from a large bowl. Nothing good, Charity was sure of that.

She got out of the car with the huge bag of candy she'd bought at the store. She turned at the sound of another vehicle. A UPS truck lumbered to a stop beside her. "Got a package for you," Chuck the UPS man called down to her from his truck.

The deputy had climbed out and come around to her side of the car. "Here," she said, shoving the bag of candy at the deputy. "Get up there on the porch and save my windows."

The deputy took the bag and hurried up the steps as Chuck held out his clipboard. "Need your signature right there, Charity."

She signed and he handed her a large cardboard envelope. Wishing her a happy Halloween, he hopped back into the truck and took off down the street as the first drops of rain began to fall again.

It wasn't until then that she looked at what he'd given her. Even in the dim light, she could read the sender's name: Nina Monroe. Charity's hands began to shake as she tore the parcel open to find a small white envelope inside with her name on it.

Rain fell harder and she started to open the purse hanging from her shoulder to stuff the letter inside. Unfortunately she had way too much in her purse already—gun, pepper spray, handcuffs—so she quickly shoved the letter into her jacket and zipped it closed.

She'd gotten a letter from a dead woman. The letter someone had been looking for? She couldn't wait to get inside and open it, even though she knew she should wait until Mitch got there.

Behind her on the porch children chattered, and more were coming up the street. As she turned toward the house, she caught movement in the trees next to her. Her heart leaped to her throat as a huge dark object came flying out of the trees like a giant bat.

But it was only a person in a hooded black cape, the face a grotesque rubbery mask. Her first thought was that it was one of the parents taking his kids trick-or-treating, someone she knew, someone just trying to scare her.

But she was too scared to speak when he grabbed her and tried to rip her coat open. It took her only an instant to realize that he was after the letter.

She screamed and fought him off, managing to break free. She could see the deputy trying to get through the cluster of kids to her.

But another cluster of kids had just started up the stairs to the porch, and the caped man was on her again. She fought him, clawing at his eyes, managing to pull his mask away for an instant. Just long enough to see his face. Bud Farnsworth! The foreman at Dennison Ducks.

She opened her mouth to scream again, but he clamped his gloved hand over her mouth and, lifting her, ran into the trees and darkness as the rain began to fall in a torrent.

Only a few yards into the forest, Charity looked back and couldn't see the house. Or anyone chasing them. They'd disappeared from view. She could hear the deputy behind them. But without a flashlight, he couldn't see her. She tried to scream but was prevented by the thick glove over her mouth. She heard the deputy on his radio calling Mitch. But how would Mitch ever be able to find her?

She struggled to free herself, but Bud was much stronger than she was, and now that she'd seen his face, she knew he'd never let her go.

He burst out of the trees onto a side road and carried her toward a black pickup. *The* black pickup. Jerking open the driver's side, he threw her in, then climbed in after her. Her purse strap broke, and several of the lighter items in it spilled across the seat. He grabbed the purse and threw it behind the seat, then hit the automatic door locks as she lunged for the opposite-side door handle. Trapped, she screamed bloody murder.

"Stupid bitch," he snarled, and backhanded her so hard she saw stars. The pickup engine roared to life. He hit the gas and tore off, tires screaming. In the side mirror, she thought she glimpsed the deputy run out into the street a block away, but Bud quickly turned and sped down the road toward Dennison Ducks.

"Give me the letter," he ordered, and ripped the mask from his face, throwing it to the floor. "Now." He backhanded her again when she didn't respond.

She cowered as close to her door as she could, crossing her arms over chest, the feel of the letter against her breast.

"Just give me the letter," he growled. "Don't make me take it from you."

Something deep inside her told her he would kill her once he got the letter. Whatever Nina had written was incriminating enough that it had cost at least one other person his life. If Charity gave Bud the letter, he would get away with murder. If she didn't, she had no doubt he would take it. Either way she was a dead woman unless she could get away from him.

Ahead she saw the turnoff for Dennison Ducks. She knew that if he took her past there, he would have her in an isolated area where she wouldn't stand a chance. In the side mirror, she saw that there were no lights in pursuit.

She was on her own.

She lunged for the steering wheel and jerked it toward the right. She heard his curse and felt the pickup swerve before he swung at her. She ducked back and felt something bite into her hip.

When her shoulder bag had spilled across the seat, the heavy items, like her gun and pepper spray, had stayed in the purse. Just her luck. Right now the handcuffs were digging into her hip. Why couldn't something useful have fallen out of her purse?

Bud fought to keep the pickup on the slippery muddy road, got it back under control and tromped down on the gas. ''I was going to wait until we were farther up the road but…'' He unlocked the doors and reached across her, grabbing the door handle. The door swung open and she saw what he planned to do. Throw her out! And at this speed, she was toast.

She reached under her hip for the handcuffs.

He grabbed the front of her jacket, trying to get the letter. Once he did…

"I'll give you the letter!" she cried, knocking his hands away.

He shifted his gaze back and forth between her and the road, not slowing down, but keeping his hands to himself. Did he think she didn't realize he still planned to throw her out the moment she handed him the letter?

A less-than-inspired plan leaped to mind. Amazing what the mind can come up with when you're totally panicked and fighting for your life.

It was suicidal. Her craziest plan yet. She reached into her jacket and then pretended to be jostled by the road. She fell toward him.

He grabbed the steering wheel with both hands, obviously thinking she was going to try to wrest it from his grip again. She reached over her head and snapped one cuff to his right wrist, planning to snap the other to the steering wheel.

The original plan had been simple, wreck the pickup and run. If she could run. And if he didn't run after her too quickly. This improved plan was even better. Bud wouldn't be able to run after her because he would be handcuffed to the steering wheel.

Bud was going ballistic, screaming at the sight of the handcuff dangling from his wrist and trying to hit her. But she had hold of the other cuff and was hanging on for dear life.

She grabbed the steering wheel, trying to hook the other cuff to it. The pickup began to swerve.

Bud knocked her away, breaking her hold on the

other cuff. The pickup was skidding sideways in the mud. Bud was fighting to keep it on the road.

With both his hands busy, she tried again, only to have him grab her by the hair and hold her down with one hand as he tried to right the pickup.

From her position facedown on the seat between the two of them, she couldn't reach the steering wheel. Her inspired plan took on a new twist, this one truly suicidal, but she'd run out of options and knew after this Bud would kill her and take the letter, then dump her body along the road and Mitch would find her in some ditch.

She snapped the other cuff to her own wrist—just an instant before the pickup careened off the road and came to a bone-jarring stop. Her head smacked the gearshift and the lights went out.

CHARITY AWOKE aware that she was being carried, the ground uneven, then flat. She opened her eyes. Rain fell on her face. There was no light at first. Then she saw the small glow at the employee entrance of Dennison Ducks. He was taking her to the plant.

At the door, he stopped to set her down, sweating from the effort of hauling her. ''I should kill you right now,'' he said, waving a gun at her with his free hand. ''Nina was much easier to kill than you. But then, Ethel had already coldcocked her good with a decoy.''

She could tell he wanted to shoot her, but he was already winded from carrying her. He needed her to walk to wherever they were going. Otherwise, she'd already be dead.

He dug out his key, cursing her, then opened the door and shoved her through it. The handcuff chaffed her wrist painfully as she stumbled inside and he jerked her back to him.

She looked around for a weapon. Her purse was in the pickup and she could see nothing within reach that she could use as he dragged her back through the shelves of ducks, never letting her get close enough to grab one. It grew darker and darker as they moved away from the light near the entrance.

At the back of the building, Bud turned on a small lamp over a workbench, picked up a hacksaw and, with the sweep of his free arm, cleared off everything within her reach.

When he turned to look at her, his face was distorted in anger. "I can't believe you did something so stupid," he spat at her as he dragged her closer to the workbench. Dropping the hacksaw, he grabbed the front of her jacket and jerked her to him. He ripped the jacket apart and the letter fell to the floor.

He stared down at it for a moment as if surprised Nina had really written it. Or maybe just surprised at what he'd had to go through to get it.

Pulling Charity down with him, he retrieved the letter from the floor. She watched him open it, dying to see what was inside. What could be in the letter that was worth killing over? Surely not Nina's true paternity. Who cared after twenty-seven years?

It had to have something to do with Angela's kidnapping. "*You* kidnapped Angela!"

"Prove it." Bud curled a lip at her, then pulled a lighter from his pocket, flicked it on and touched the flame to the paper without even a glance in her direction.

"No!" she cried, grabbing for the letter. But it was too late. The paper caught fire in an instant, and as he dropped it to the floor, the flame turned what was left of the letter to ash.

She wanted to cry. But she had much worse problems. Bud had disposed of the letter. Now all he had to do was dispose of her. No one would suspect him, after all. The deputy who'd seen him grab her had only seen a man in a mask and cape driving a black pickup. Even with Rogers dead, no one would know it had been Bud behind the wheel.

Bud was going to get away not only with Angela's kidnapping but with two murders.

She told herself that Mitch would get here. The deputy had called him. Mitch would find the black pickup in the ditch. He would find her. Eventually.

Bud picked up the hacksaw and seemed to realize he couldn't both cut with the saw and hold the gun on her. He moved the gun out of her reach, shifted the hacksaw to his left hand and clumsily began to saw on the metal between the two cuffs, cursing a blue streak as he did.

Her mind raced. She knew that once he got the cuffs apart that would be it for her. She could try to run, but there was no doubt in her mind he would shoot her down. And what were the chances of any-one's coming here on Halloween night? She couldn't depend on Mitch's getting here in time, either.

She listened to the grating of the saw, horrified to see how quickly the blade was cutting through the metal. Must have been cheap handcuffs.

"You know you're not going to get away with this," she said.

He shot her a look that said that line only worked in movies. Of course he was going to get away with it.

Over the rasp of the saw, she thought she heard a sound, a soft *whoosh* like a door opening. Mitch? No. If it really was the door opening, then it had to be someone with a key.

Something moved at the window next to her. A shadow. She glanced out of the corner of her eye, but saw only a tree limb brush against the glass. Just her imagination. Just like the sound of a door open-ing?

Bud was working at the handcuff. A few more mo-ments and he would be free of her. She needed to make her move the second the cuffs came apart....

That was when she smelled wet night air. Someone *had* come in through the employee door. Bud didn't seem to have noticed.

She couldn't see who'd entered the plant because of the fully stocked shelves.

The saw cut through the link of metal that con-nected them. In that instant, Charity lunged for one of the decoys on the shelves off to her left and her hand closed around a drake's neck. She stepped back toward Bud and swung, catching him in the temple before he could pick up the gun. The gun fell, skittering across the concrete and sliding under one of the shelves.

He stumbled back and she turned to run, only to find herself staring into the business end of another gun. Holding it was the last person she'd expected to see.

"Daisy?"

Her theory about Daisy hiring someone to get rid of Angela suddenly came back to her in a rush.

"Don't move," Daisy ordered, pointing the gun at Bud now. Daisy's gaze moved to the ashes on the floor at his feet. "So you got to the letter and destroyed it." Her gaze was hard as stones.

Charity held her breath, not sure Daisy wouldn't kill her if she moved. If Daisy really had hired Bud to kidnap Angela, then why was she pointing the gun at him? Unless she planned to kill him to keep him quiet. With Nina dead and the letter gone...

"Nina told me she knew who kidnapped Angela," Daisy was saying. "I thought she was bluffing. She said lucky for me she loved revenge even more than money and that she'd written a letter to the newspaper. Charity would get it on Halloween and the masks would be off. I guess the mask is off, Bud."

Bud licked his lips and looked nervously around.

"Where is the private investigator I hired?" Daisy asked. "I saw his truck..."

"He's dead," Charity offered. "Bud was driving

the truck. He was getting ready to kill me when you came in.''

Daisy didn't seem to hear. She narrowed her gaze at Bud and said, ''Where is my daughter?'' Her eerie calm made the hair stand up on the back of Charity's neck. ''Oh God, I should have known it would be you who took my daughter. You'd do anything for money. Where is Angela?''

''I don't know, I swear to God, Daisy.'' Bud was leaning against the workbench as if his knees wouldn't hold him. ''I sold her to some lawyer. He never gave me his name.''

Bud glanced behind Daisy as if he saw something in the darkness by the decoy shelves. Or someone. Fear distorted his face. He was shaking his head as if suddenly more afraid.

Charity saw what he planned to do. She opened her mouth, but it happened too fast. Bud dived for his gun, which had slid under a decoy shelf.

He came up with it, rolling and firing at Daisy. The air boomed with gunfire and the smell of gunpowder met Charity's nostrils.

Charity saw Daisy stagger, her shoulder blooming with red as she crumpled to the floor. Then she heard Bud cry out as another shot exploded.

In the same instant, the window shattered behind her, showering her with glass. She was knocked to the floor and Mitch was there.

Then Charity was in Mitch's arms and he was holding her close and she was crying as he stroked her hair and whispered, ''It's okay, baby. It's okay.''

And Wade was there, rushing to Daisy's side, a gun in his hand. Charity was the only one to see Bud's expression. He was looking at Wade and trying to speak, but no words came out as he clutched his chest where he'd been shot, and died.

Epilogue

In the days that followed, the talk at Betty's was about nothing but the murders—and the twenty-seven-year-old kidnapping. Another Bigfoot sighting on the edge of town went by barely noticed.

Mitch had pieced the story together as best he could for Charity. Nina had been planning to meet Wade at the decoy plant Tuesday night, but instead, Ethel Whiting had shown up. They'd fought and Ethel had hit Nina, knocking her unconscious.

Bud had been outside, planning to kill Nina. He'd found her, killed her and dumped her and her car in the ravine. The problem was, he wouldn't have been able to do that without help. Maybe his wife had driven the second car. She wasn't talking. In fact, she was packing, moving away from Timber Falls. Or maybe it had been someone else in town. Charity wondered if they would ever know the truth.

Bud had killed Nina to keep her from exposing his part in Angela's kidnapping. At least that was the theory. Charity had one of her own. If Bud had kidnapped Angela for money, then he could have killed Nina for the person behind the kidnapping.

Or there could have been no conspiracy at all, Mitch reminded her. Maybe along with Wade, Nina had been blackmailing Bud. Only, Bud was never planning to pay.

Daisy was recovering from a gunshot wound to her shoulder at a hospital in Eugene. When Charity went down to visit her, the room was full of flowers from residents of Timber Falls. Shooting Bud Farnsworth had gotten her back into the town's good graces, it seemed. People were willing to give her another chance.

"Did you see the letter before he burned it?" Daisy asked her.

Charity had to tell her she didn't. "I don't think Nina knew where Angela was." She wasn't sure if that had been the case, but she thought it would make things easier for Daisy, who'd hired Kyle Rogers to get the letter—if Nina really had written a letter to get her revenge like she'd told Daisy she planned to do. But all Rogers had gotten was killed for it. And no one would ever know now what Nina had written Charity about the kidnapping or Bud Farnsworth.

DNA tests had confirmed that Wade was indeed Nina's father. Charity had heard that Desiree hadn't taken it well. It was hard to say how Daisy took the news. She still seemed too calm to Charity, like a woman on the edge, barely hanging on.

When Wade entered the hospital room, Charity left. She couldn't forget Bud's fear just before he'd gone for his gun. Or his attempt to speak to Wade at the very end of his life. She still had nightmares.

Mitch had been sleeping on her couch in the weeks since. She'd decided it was all right to show a man that she needed him. At least for a while.

Ethel hadn't gone back to work at Dennison Ducks even after Wade apologized to her and she was released on bond, trial pending. No one thought she would get any jail time. Wade was advertising for a new secretary. Charity's newspaper circulation had increased and she was actually showing a pretty good profit. But she had realized something. Mitch didn't care if she wrote a Pulitzer prize-winning story or not. How about that?

On her way back from visiting Daisy at the hospital in Eugene, she drove into town in time for a late breakfast at Betty's Café.

Betty slid a piece of banana-cream pie and a diet cola in front of her as she took her usual stool.

"See that guy over there?" Betty whispered.

Charity turned to see a dark-haired man in his thirties sitting in the far booth poring over a stack of papers. He wasn't bad-looking. But he was no Mitch Tanner.

"He looks too stodgy for you," Charity said, turning back to her pie. "Anyway, I thought you were seeing that new bartender at the Duck-In."

Betty blushed. "Bruno? Who told you that?"

Charity just laughed. "Don't tell me that's Bruno over there."

"No, he's that scientist—the one who did that horrible article on Liam Sawyer. Said the photos Liam took all those years ago of Bigfoot were just part of an elaborate hoax.''

Ford Lancaster. Charity glanced over her shoulder at him. ''So what's he doing in town?''

''That's just it,'' Betty said. ''No one knows. I guess it's probably this latest Bigfoot sighting, but I wonder if it could have anything to do with Liam being back in town.''

Charity certainly hoped not. She didn't want to see her friend Roz hurt anymore by all that old stuff about her father. ''So tell me about your latest heartache in blue jeans.''

The bell over the door tinkled.

''Speaking of heartache,'' Betty said under her breath, then called out, ''Good mornin', Sheriff. Saved you a piece of banana-cream.''

''No pie for me this morning, Betty.'' Mitch slid onto the stool next to Charity, and Betty placed a cup of black coffee in front of him before disappearing discreetly into the back.

''GOOD MORNING, Charity.'' Mitch looked over at her and felt his heart leap at just the sight of her. It was overcast outside, clouds low and gray, rain threatening again. But it was like there was sunlight all around her. Her auburn hair seemed on fire this morning, and her face seemed to light up like springtime.

He told himself it was the banana-cream pie, not him.

"Morning, Sheriff." She took a bite of pie, closed her eyes and smiled. He hadn't seen her smile in days and felt a rush of pure pleasure just watching her.

She opened her eyes. "Care for a bite?"

Oh, he was tempted. But not by banana-cream pie. In the days since he'd crashed through a glass window to save Charity, he'd thought a lot about the two of them. He didn't know how he felt about anything—just that he couldn't stay away from her. Didn't want to.

Not that he wasn't still scared. Last night he'd had dinner with his father and Jesse. It hadn't been all that bad. He was trying to see the man that Jesse had always known. It would take time.

But he wasn't as afraid of himself. He'd always worried he was too much like his father. Now he wasn't so sure that was a bad thing.

As for Charity… "I was wondering…" His mouth was dry as cotton. He took a sip of coffee. "Do you have any plans for this weekend?"

She raised a brow in surprise.

"Saturday night. I was thinking…" That old voice in his head tried to stop him, but he wasn't listening anymore. "Maybe you'd like to go to the community-center dance. We could have dinner first."

Charity was speechless. It was always something to behold. "Are you asking me for a…date?"

"I believe I am."

She grinned. "Well, you're in luck. I just happen to be free Saturday."

He reached into his pocket, feeling bashful, as he

set the box with the bracelet on the counter. "I thought you might want to wear this."

Her eyes were big as pie plates when she saw the bracelet she'd eyed at the Eugene jewelry store. "Oh, Mitch." Tears welled in those eyes and she bit her lower lip. Then she kissed him.

He felt himself falling, out of control, falling, only this time it didn't seem quite so frightening. But then he saw himself clear as day in a black tuxedo standing at an altar, and next to him—

"It's just a dance," he said when the kiss ended.

Charity smiled that secret smile of hers. "Whatever you say, Mitch."

HARLEQUIN®
INTRIGUE®

has a new lineup of books to keep you on
the edge of your seat throughout the winter.
So be on the alert for…

BACHELORS AT LARGE

**Bold and brash—these men have sworn to serve
and protect as officers of the law…and only the
most special women can "catch" these good guys!**

UNDER HIS PROTECTION
BY AMY J. FETZER
(October 2003)

UNMARKED MAN
BY DARLENE SCALERA
(November 2003)

BOYS IN BLUE
A special 3-in-1 volume with
REBECCA YORK (Ruth Glick writing as Rebecca York),
ANN VOSS PETERSON AND PATRICIA ROSEMOOR
(December 2003)

CONCEALED WEAPON
BY SUSAN PETERSON
(January 2004)

GUARDIAN OF HER HEART
BY LINDA O. JOHNSTON
(February 2004)

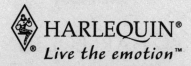

HARLEQUIN®
Live the emotion™

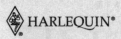

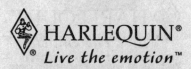

eHARLEQUIN.com

The eHarlequin.com online community is *the* place to share opinions, thoughts and feelings!

- Joining the community is easy, fun and **FREE!**

- Connect with **other romance fans** on our message boards.

- Meet your **favorite authors** without leaving home!

- **Share opinions** on books, movies, celebrities…and *more!*

Here's what our members say:

"I love the friendly and helpful atmosphere filled with support and humor."
—Texanna (eHarlequin.com member)

"Is this the place for me, or what? There is nothing I love more than 'talking' books, especially with fellow readers who are reading the same ones I am."
—Jo Ann (eHarlequin.com member)

Join today by visiting www.eHarlequin.com!

If you enjoyed what you just read,
then we've got an offer you can't resist!

Take 2 bestselling love stories FREE!

Plus get a FREE surprise gift!

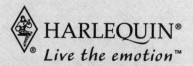